How I Gave My Heart to the Restaurant Business

Also by Karen Hubert Allison

The Vegetarian Compass (A Cookbook)

Horror, Adventure, Mystery and Romance in the American Class-room: Teaching and Writing Popular Fiction

In Search of Fred and Ethel Mertz (Poetry)

How I Gave My Heart to the Restaurant Business

A Novel by
Karen Hubert Allison

THE ECCO PRESS

THE ECCO PRESS
100 West Broad Street
Hopewell, New Jersey 08525
Published simultaneously in Canada by
Penguin Books Canada Ltd., Ontario
Printed in the United States of America
Library of Congress Cataloging-in-Publication Data
Allison, Karen Hubert.
    How I gave my heart to the restaurant business : a novel / by Karen
Hubert Allison. — 1st Ecco ed.
        p.   cm.
    ISBN 0-88001-522-5
    I. Title.
PS3551.L455H69   1997
813'.54 — dc20   96-41680
Designed by Angela Foote Design
The text of this book is set in Galliard
9 8 7 6 5 4 3 2 1
FIRST EDITION

For my husband Len Allison

with gratitude to Emily Anne Black Gargiulo
and in memory of Dr. Ernest Angel and Leo Lerman

How I Gave My Heart to the Restaurant Business

One

"Born to eat, born to cook," Slav Czesny, astrologer, sighed as he looked up from his ephemeris. "Any road you take will lead you back to food. Sun, Venus and Mercury in Virgo at the midheaven." Slav looked up at me from behind his bifocals, shrugging. "For better or worse, from now on, your life is a soup bone."

The cosmic checkup confirmed what I already suspected. We were sitting in my kitchen. I lived in a railroad flat in the East Village where I had a sunny front room I used as my studio, a bedroom and a large purple and green kitchen with a bathtub big enough for keeping lobsters alive overnight. I was three months away from earning my Master of Fine Arts, trying to finish enough canvases to mount an exhibition of still lifes that would stand as my thesis: sweating apples, oozing cheese, crumbling breads. The completed paintings hung on the wall: *Napoleons for My Mother, Figs Seducing Baked Apple, Canadian Cheddar Meets Slab Bacon, Hot Chocolate and Custard Pie Discuss the News.* As for the dozen unfinished canvases, it seemed that every time I sat down to paint, I got up to cook instead.

By the age of twenty-four I had already fricasseed my way through Julia, volumes I and II, flirted with vegetarianism, fallen in love with beef marrow, goose liver, port wine and triple cream cheeses. I had uncovered the secrets of pâte brisée and worn out the treads of my pasta machine.

I had been bred for a life of gallery shmoozing, not cooking. My parents, through hard work, sacrifice and clever deal-making, had successfully pursued a lifetime of collecting and selling early twentieth-century art. Some parents wish for a boy, others for a doctor or lawyer. Mine wanted an artist. I had hoped Slav would predict a future both my mother and I could live with.

Slav's heavy-lidded eyes bulged with the urgency of celestial information. He looked up at me through his bifocals, hummed and agreed with himself. He was absorbed in the configuration of my planets, spread out like stellar Rorschachs.

"Moon in Taurus. House of comfort, digestion, rich foods." He leaned closer. "Wake up, you silly girl, and smell the baguettes. Change is in the wind, Kitterina Kittridge." He closed his worn book. "Culminates in a year or two. A few rough spots down the pike after that, but it won't last. You'll always be able to stir a pot and make a buck. You were born with food in your fingers. Born to eat, born to cook."

Instead of painting, I was a foodie madwoman caught up in a cooking frenzy. I spent the whole week planning my Saturday night dinner parties when I invited graduate students and teachers to my home and cooked my heart out for them. It didn't matter that I wasn't much of a conversationalist, that I dried up like zwieback when guests discussed political issues or their root canal operations. I didn't have to talk, I cooked. People were happy at my dinner parties. Lovers cuddled and danced, friends got drunk and arm wrestled, advertising majors argued politics. I transported them all, via boeuf en daube with caramelized parsnips, to the streets of Paris, and with bigoli al ragu di polpi, to the canals of Venice. One weekend I served rich Czarist Russian fare; the next, post-revolutionary pirogies and roasted root vegetables as a paean to Marx.

"So, you see me with a nice little cozy cafe somewhere in the country?" Gingham curtains, colorful linen, flowers on every table, an original menu, grateful guests.

"I see a shiny asteroid in New York's current culinary galaxy. I see money, success in the fifth house."

At the end of our reading, I could almost taste the direction my life was about to take, I could almost see what the universe had in store for me, though it never occurred to me to leave school and cook for a living. But a few days later, my next-door neighbor Wally saw God in my kitchen, and that changed everything.

Wally never missed my dinner parties. He ate hungrily, lavished compliments, and was the only guest who ever brought me flowers. Wally loved to eat, but all he knew about cooking was to throw everything he had into one pot and cook it for eight hours. He called it La Boheme stew, and he ate it out of the pot all week long.

Walter Willicott III was tall and handsome with sandy hair and eyes that changed from blue to cloudy gray. He had a healthy, athletic body, owned a cat named the General, and lived in a disorderly apartment he cleaned once a month by opening wide all his windows regardless of the season or temperature. These aerations had a kind of restorative effect on him, and afterwards he was always happier and calmer. We were next-door neighbors on the fifth floor of the same walk-up tenement. It was a clean, well-kept block, dominated by Ukrainians who had brought up generations of children in small, chain-like apartments passed down carefully like family jewels.

Unlike myself, Walter lived the clichéd life of an artist: his cramped rooms were filled with rolled canvases and the smell of oil paint. He cultivated eccentric habits, expressed emotional highs and despairs, gave wild parties, and disdained authority. For all this, Wally was the worst painter in the world, but he loved making art with a passion I had never known.

Talented or not, he offered to paint my portrait in return for all the meals I'd fed him. I had no use for his paintings, which I considered inferior in every way to mine, so I flatly refused to pose for him. Wally painted me anyway, while I cooked in my kitchen, preparing Saturday dinner. He worked on it for several weekends. I didn't mind because I liked company while I cooked, even the kind that Wally offered. He was much funnier than the radio. Wally was full of advice and one-liners as he painted me. He quoted the Beatles and Schopenhauer and gave pedantic speeches about politics and art. Always art. He ranted art history, raved art criticism, took issue with biographers of artists whose lives he admired. He jabbered on imperiously about Lautrec, Degas. He insisted he had blood ties to Browning, emotional ties to Rembrandt, spiritual ties to Gauguin. And when the portrait was done it was just as ugly as all the rest of his work. Still, I was touched when he asked that I hang the painting in my kitchen.

"Where your heart is," he explained.

One Saturday night after a group of us had eaten, Wally renamed me. He stood on a chair in my kitchen and called for the guests to be quiet. Wally the arrogant toasted my stove as he waved his lifted wineglass at my glass cabinets stocked with ingredients and dishes. "*This* is your life's work. Forget painting; it's more angst per square inch, anyway. It's a sideline compared to the work you do in here. To *Kitchie*," he said, and afterwards the name stuck.

Wally believed in the redemptive suffering of artists, a notion I couldn't stomach. I knew perfectly well the relationship between making art and making money, and Wally would have none of it. I found his concept of the-artist-as-sufferer as boring as mashed potatoes. I, who was very good at making art if school grades were any measure, never did it, and he, who was patently untalented, desperately toiled away all the time. Painting was a burdensome family mantle I had inherited, like unwanted wealth or title. I had been made to feel I had a certain responsibility to it, to *the talent* as my mother called it, as though it had its own life within me. I felt obligated. I had grown up as an altar girl in the New York Cathedral of Art. Poor Wally was a storefront Baptist by comparison.

My parents collected Henry, Jackson, Davies, Bellows, artists blown into obscurity by the Armory show of 1912, affordable investments for some decades after. Lilly and Theo lived for their ever-expanding collection, were most alive when contemplating a purchase. They had not started out as people of means, but in time their flourishing collection was worth a great deal of money, more than one would expect to be amassed by a bookkeeper and his wife who managed a lingerie department in Macy's. They had brown-bagged it to work every day of their working lives and invested every cent of their modest salaries in art. Until I was a teenager, we did not go to movies, take vacations, or eat out. By then, Lilly and Theo were known around galleries as two of the shrewdest collectors of

American paintings in New York. My father died soon after achieving that, and with the money she received from his life insurance, Lilly went on to make some of her greatest deals, increasing her net worth substantially.

As a child, I viewed their growing collection suspiciously, like an unwanted sibling. I was raised as an art zombie, and comparisons could be drawn between the training I received under my mother's hopeful eye to the training of young ballet dancers who practice until their little toes bleed. When I was eight years old Albers' color theories were being read to me as bedtime stories. I knew the difference between gouache and watercolor, as well as the feel of a real sable brush. There were classes and seminars at the museum school and every Saturday morning and Thursday afternoon I attended an anatomy and figure-drawing class, in which I was the only child. On one occasion, my fifth grade teacher, Mrs. MacWhirley, asked those of us who left early on Thursdays for religious instruction to raise their hands. I raised mine. As she wrote our names on a list, she called on me and asked, "Immaculate Conception or Temple Beth Shalom?"

"Art Students League," I answered.

Wally painted me standing at a yellow stove cooking with purple pots. My hands, a watery fleshy pink, bled into a bunch of orange carrots as though my fingers had melted into vegetables. My cheeks were high and full. "You're always chewing, so I made you look like a squirrel," he explained.

Wally's portrait of me as a cooking squirrel was not the result of painterly intention, but of limited ability to render a face attached to a body. I wish I could say that there was some raw, abrasive energy in Wally's paintings, or vivid color and brash technique, but the only thing that shone through his work was dogged insistence.

Most times, my friendship with Wally had nothing to do with art. It was more about that borrow-a-cup-of-sugar thing that exists between neighbors, especially single ones. If we were both up at 2:00 A.M., we would visit and talk. We collected mail, accepted packages, traded errands, picked up groceries, loaned irons, took shirts to the Chinese laundry for each other. We were more like brother and sister than conveniently placed artists.

Wally became the unofficial host of all my Saturday night dinner parties. A great storyteller, he had a handy supply of jokes, an ample collection of the controversial, an inexhaustible number of stunning facts of the believe-it-or-not kind most often encountered at barside. It was not for the purposes of information-gathering that Wally spent so much of his time in bars. The son of two alcoholics, he was raised by his aunt, a famous psychiatrist who specialized in treating alcoholics. Aunt Dorian kept Wally in a constant supply of Antabuse pills which he took each day. Unless he was off on a bender. Wally was the only son of Aunt Dorian's youngest and favorite brother, Wally Jr., who had died an alcoholic death. Wally's mother, a wild woman in her day, had managed to live out her marginal but dry life in a Salvation Army residence in the city. It took all of Wally's mother's energy not to drink. There was nothing left over with which to raise a child, so custody of Wally was given to Aunt Dorian, who was busy with her medical practice. And so, young Walter grew up treated to round-the-clock nannies.

Doses of money and private schools, blue blazers and French lessons did not change what his aunt referred to as Wally's *chro-*

mosomal pool. "Genes. Runs in the family," his aunt confided when we first met. "If you see him drinking, just call me," she added and handed me her card. At a tender age, Wally had found the keys to the liquor closet and was diagnosed by Aunt Dorian as an official alcoholic by the time he hit junior high school. Even though he was now grown and out of college, Aunt Dorian policed him at least once a month. Whenever Aunt Dorian dropped by to check on her nephew, she slid a card under my door. Being policed by older women was something Wally and I had in common. While Wally's aunt was hot on his trail for liquor on his breath, my mother made routine visits to my studio to chart my all-too-slow progress towards the full-blown artistic career she intended to manage for me.

Wally, a few years older than me and a graduate of Bard College, lived off a modest trust fund his aunt had set up for him, enough to cover food and rent. For everything else, including art supplies, Wally had to scramble. This was where Wally was an original. His most imaginative effort was his "Send a Young Artist to Mexico" campaign. His old classmates (whose monthly trust fund checks came to far more than his) paid to send him to Puerto Vallarta one summer in exchange for free paintings. Just as I would always have food in my life, Wally Willicott III would never be short on people to care for him.

For the most part, during the three years Wally and I were neighbors, he was off the wagon. He would socialize with me when he wasn't drinking, and when he was he would all but disappear from my sight for days or weeks. I could hear shrieks of laughter and strange celebrations from his apartment next door. An odd assortment of strangers would go in and out of his apartment all day and until late at night. Just as he lived a studied cliché of an artist's life when he was sober, Wally lived the cliché of the cheerful, carousing drunk when he was drinking.

It was during one of Wally's longest and worst drunks that I found myself unable to finish the last three canvases for my Master's thesis. I had tried to work, but why paint an apple when you could eat it? Besides, Slav had left me with the impression that I might as well never paint again. I wondered if I had cooked the art out of me. It had paled, like a beet that's lost its color to a boiling soup.

On the day my art career officially hit the dust, I was already a month past the second extension of my thesis deadline. I had suggested to the chairman of the M.F.A. program that the painting department let me cater its spring party in place of the missing canvases. "I could photograph my cooking and maybe I could present it as a happening, or as edible art, or how about half and half?" The chairman urged my watercolor professor, Franklyn Mist (a man who loved my eclairs), to visit my studio and talk some sense, or some art, into me. Franklyn was a bear of a man at almost seven feet tall, and loved by students for his course *How To Find Your Empty Space and Paint It*. A watercolorist, he painted the space around trees and in between branches, and never worked on paper larger than twelve inches.

It was a beautiful morning, a pure blue winter light, good for painting, if you're painting. The stuff of still lifes, bread, bottles and fruit, were arranged on separate tables all over my studio. I waited for Franklyn to arrive as the sun drenched the walls, the radiator hissed, and the shriveling melons and pineapples fermented like overripe fruit salad. I sipped coffee out of a turquoise mug, worrying less about the fate of my unfinished canvases and more about whether Franklyn would like the scones I planned to serve him, when the banging in Wally's apartment started again.

The noise had started at the beginning of Wally's current bender. It had started the usual way, with his disappearance for a few nights, then his return home, holding long, loud parties with one or two other drunks, a few reasonably happy screeches with possible sexual overtones, and then of course I had found the General meowing, hungry, in the hallway. I had let him into my apartment and had been feeding him now for about a week. None of this seemed particularly different from Wally's behavior in the past. Except for that banging. At first it had a nice rhythmic pattern to it. Very Zen of Wally to make such orderly noise. But then the hammering went on for days, while the breaks in between grew shorter. I wondered if he had taken his new love affair with Rodin to heart, if he had turned to sculpting. Perhaps a change in metier would help Wally to produce things that looked good.

I stood the hammering for as long as I could, and on the third night I disobeyed our unwritten agreement not to interrupt each other when one of us was working. Even Brancusi had to get some sleep. It was after midnight. He had to stop. I broke our code. I knocked. And knocked. And knocked.

Wally opened the door suspiciously. He wore a strange, frightened expression and would not open the door fully. His eyes darted back and forth, and he was unshaven. He kept the chain on.

"Who is it?" he asked, looking straight at me.

"Kitchie."

What was this business with the chain? Who was he keeping out?

"Are you all right?" I asked. "Do you want some tea or soup or something?"

"None of the above," he said. "Have to go now. Company's calling."

I had heard no one go in or out for days.

"Wally, listen, I hate to complain, but all the hammering, I can't get to sleep. Please—"

His eyes widened. They seemed grayer and cloudier than usual, the pupils like black rivets. He had the grizzly makings of a red beard.

"I know," he whispered, "it's driving me crazy too. Any idea who's doing it?"

"Come on, Wal," I said, smiling at his obvious invitation to a cat-mouse game. "I know you're sculpting in there."

He unhooked the chain, squeezed through a narrow opening of the door, and ventured out into the hallway. Still careful not to let me look inside. He looked past me towards the stairwell, as though he were afraid someone he didn't want to see might be coming up.

Then he abruptly put his arms around me and hugged me tightly, squashing my face against his chest. He pulled me away, held me at arm's length, and looked at me with gratitude.

"Kitchie, Kitchie, Kitchie." He shook his head as though I'd just answered some metaphysical question he'd been wrestling with. "That's it exactly! I'm a sculptor. A goddamn sculptor."

He let me go and drew himself up, a breath deeper, an inch taller.

"Space is *so eternal*. But you know all about what's important. You're a *feeder*. A natural-born cook." Then he patted my arm. A look of beatific largesse came over his face.

"You're a *tit*, Kitchie. An eternal *tit*." Then he went back in to his apartment, shut the door, locked up again, and I was left standing there in the three feet between our apartment doors, wondering if I'd really heard all that.

The banging stopped and I got some sleep that night only to be awakened early in the morning by more banging. I got up, washed, dressed, and cleaned the studio. Franklyn Mist was on his way. Scones were baking, coffee was brewing. I turned the radio on full blast, hoping to drown out some of the banging coming from Wally's studio, and waited for my advisor to arrive.

When Franklyn arrived, he was far more curious about my kitchen than my studio and took to studying my collection of copper pots and whisks. We got to talking recipes. He was hungry for a good cassoulet, and he loved the scones, but even fresh currants and a hint of anise and orange couldn't compete with the pounding that was going on next door.

"Neighbor renovating?" he asked politely.

He tried to ignore the noise, and after two cups of coffee, admitted he had come bearing bad news. The three paintings were due next week, or else. "Nix the catering idea," was how Franklyn put it. We moved on to the studio to the dried pasta still life awaiting completion. A nagging study in shapes, I called it *Vermicelli Lost on Blue Velvet*. Noodles could be tricky, I explained, especially in oils. Franklyn was about to discuss the properties of methylene blue when the pounding next door became really intolerable, even for a moon child like myself with a gift for ignoring the obvious. The banging became so loud it seemed to be closing in on us. My ears and head hurt. The rhythmic thudding and crashing had brought us both, advisor and student, to the edge of polite tolerance when suddenly Franklyn pointed at the wall of my living room which had begun to pulsate, to breathe and heave. I had a brief, mystical flash that my life as I knew it was about to end. *Change is in the wind, Kitterina Kittridge.* Slav's warning flashed as Franklyn pulled me out of the studio and we backed into the kitchen, watching as the wall between my studio and Wally's swelled out like a belly, then cracked slowly like a hard-boiled egg. Spiky fissures branched into jagged splits that grew in size until the wall caved in and cement crumbled down, clearing a hole large enough for Wally to climb through, holding the largest pickax I had ever seen.

He wore a smile of utter victory and confidence. Sporting his new beard, long johns and ski jacket, Wally looked like a cross between Nanook of the North and Admiral Perry in thermals, whomping his way through ice to get to the last vestige of unexplored territory left on earth.

"Well," he sighed, relieved, as though he had finally reached the Pole.

"There *He* is." He held the blade of the ax in his hand and pointed the tool's wooden end towards my stove.

"Right where I thought *He'd* be." Wally smiled his fearless, self-congratulatory, arrogant smile and looked right past us to the stove in the corner.

"Standing right here, in your kitchen." His eyes started filling up the way they did whenever he talked art foolishness. I never took his tears seriously. It was just Wally being Wally. But this time his penchant for the dramatic had gone too far, and I was about to tell him so when he pointed his ax again and said, "*God* is standing in *your* kitchen, over by the pot rack, you lucky woman."

There stood Wally, covered with plaster dust, full of the vision of God. It would have been very hard to say whether Wally was more impressed with me for having such special company or himself for discovering the divine and seeing the invisible.

The three of us were locked in a spiritual face-off, a moment of divine reckoning. Who would do what next? My poor friend was nuts and had just crossed over into a personal twilight zone. On the other hand, I was still young enough to think that such spiritual gibberish might be visionary. I still believed enough in magic so that all I could think was: *If God has taken up residence in my kitchen, why the hell am I the last one to know about it?*

Franklyn waited with me until the ambulance came. He took the two extra scones I wrapped up for him and waved a solemn goodbye as the siren wailed and took Wally and me off to Saint Vincent's Hospital. I rode with him and held his hand. I stroked his forehead and said reassuring things. Meanwhile he kept repeating, savoring the wonder of it, that he had seen God. He admonished me, wasn't I the lucky duck to have entertained The Great One at a spiritual power breakfast in my apple-green and purple kitchen.

In time Wally got better.

"You mustn't take Antabuse and drink alcohol at the same time, dear," cautioned Aunt Dorian.

When I had returned from the hospital that afternoon, I saw the building had been cordoned off. I looked up and saw a gaping hole where the two windows to Wally's apartment ought to have been. I understood it was just one of Wally's aerations gone too far, a crazy person's version of housecleaning during which Wally had disposed not only of all the plaster walls, but his two front windows. Wally was evicted after the landlord inspected his meticulous removal of plaster, walls and windows.

"I needed space, more light, I needed to let God in," he explained to me conspiratorially during one of my later hospital visits. Apparently, Wally had been entertaining the Holy Spirit of Art while removing mortar and bricks when he suddenly decided to take a break and pay me a visit through our common wall.

"You weren't using your studio," he explained, "so I figured you wouldn't mind if I came in and borrowed some of your space, you know, like a cup of sugar," he explained.

From a madman's lips come the simplest truths. Why hadn't I had the heart to see God at my stove, banging pots or stirring soup or whatever it was Wally saw him doing there? Slav had told me, but I hadn't listened. It took Wally chopping down my studio.

Truth is, I never painted again. I never lifted another brush, stretched another canvas, prepared another palette, or arranged another still life. That night I made myself an estouffade with three meats and abalone, which I had with red wine, crusty bread, a slab of St. Andre and a ripe comice pear. I ate every bit of it myself, and the next morning I bought the *New York Times*, read the Help Wanteds, went right out, and found myself a job cooking. I was willing to start at the bottom, confident that, like good cream, I would quickly rise to the top.

Two

I was waiting in the Cauldron of Peace Health Food Restaurant for a job interview with the manager. Aurora, hair plaited into a hundred dangling braids, wore Indian bracelets on her wrists and ankles and necklaces hung with mini cowbells. With Aurora walked, she rang like a telephone. We sat down at one of the restaurant's small tables made from a tree trunk.

She poured some Mu tea and asked to see my palms. She read my lines like a reference letter.

"We could use you next door at the Well of Health."

I took the job. It wasn't cooking, but, I told myself, it was a start.

I arrived early each morning to open up the Well. I took in the mail and turned the spotlight on the sign above the door that read, *Eat as though your life depended on it.* I accepted deliveries, opened burlap sacks of bulgur, brown rice and soy grits, poured them into plastic bags, weighed and sealed them with little white labels with a drawing of a well on them. I worked the cash register, swept the floor, fed the cat, and read that month's newest alternative magazine reporting on all the new UFO sightings in California. It wasn't exactly the epicurean center of the universe, but I was surrounded by food, or at least pound-size bags of it.

In a few months I had learned all I could about the soy bean and moved on to Jenks and Wolenska, Exotic Food Emporium. Jenks and Wolenska was a large, loft-like store that sold the newest and best in fancy foods, from caviar to dumplings. Our truffles came from Paris by jet, our mozzarella from bathtubs in Little Italy. No food was out of the reach of Jenks and Wolenska, no fruit too exotic (peaches you had to shave before you ate), no ingredient too rare (double yolk goose eggs for baking), no cheese too offensive (kept in a special isolation tank and removed with rubber gloves and tongs).

On Thursdays at 9:00 P.M., after the store closed, the staff were invited to stay for the weekly J&W Taster during which thirty new items were sampled. It was considered very poor form not to stay for a Thursday Taster if you wanted to get ahead at J&W. Attendance was taken and comment sheets were passed around on which opinions might be written by each taster. J&W considered itself a foodie democracy, and the results of each Taste Tally were posted in a little newsletter passed around to employees called *The Weekly Tum*.

J&W's black-and-white geometric design reminded me of a crossword puzzle. Ms. Jenks, who ruled over its wide aisles, was sharp tongued and did a lot of firing. She was a tall, thin brunette with curly hair that trailed behind her head like frisée. She was always in a hurry, her movements sharp, efficient, angular. To match the store, she wore filmy black or white garments usually held together with a bulky brooch.

By contrast, Mr. Wolenska with his round pink face was soft-spoken and boyish. He was away most of the time on buying missions. Wolenska treated the high-strung Jenks with polite forbearance, whereas the deferential Jenks was always anticipating his return and excited to welcome him back. She nervously planned teas and dinners out in his honor. For all her appearance of modernity, she was like one of those virtuous eighteenth-century wives welcoming back her seafaring captain of a husband too long at sea.

Theirs was a marriage made in business heaven. The peripatetic Wolenska filled the store with items while Jenks stayed put, beautified shelves, and sold whatever her partner brought back from his jaunts. Looking down the bulging aisles must have made Wolenska proud; at heart he was a collector, an acquisitor even more than he was a wanderer, just as surely as his partner, the redoubtable Jenks, was an arranger.

At J&W, edible style was expensive; the allure of good and plenty came in the form of thirty-dollar honey and exotic onions. Quail rested its privileged flesh on shaved ice, and Turkish figs were sold still clinging to their vines. Luxury kitchen gadgets of every kind were displayed, while rolling wooden ladders zipped musically along the artfully arranged shelves as clerks and customers climbed higher and higher to make their choices. Just by eating any one of the thousands of strange items, you could be transported to another time and place. Grapes lifted you to the steep, rocky hills of Switzerland, dark plum jam hugged you to the earthy bosom of Hungary. For every bite you took here, you needed a passport.

I had been working in this Dickensian atmosphere almost two months when my mother, after months of disapproving silence, decided to pay me a visit. My decision to become a cook was the worst thing that could have happened to Lilly, who had been intent on making me an artist. I possessed a precocious gift to render subjects realistically, though I lacked the overall vision, the soul, if you will, of an artist. At first, Lilly thought my still lifes were amusing, but she hoped I would pass on to more important subjects. When I did not, she accused me of being cavalier. If someone had trained her, she said, as carefully as she had trained me, then perhaps she would be making art instead of selling it. In the end, the talent I possessed was more Lilly's than mine. My anger about that shaped me more than a childhood of art classes ever could.

The lessons of beauty ran deep in Lilly's blood. Because Lilly had been a stunning child, her own ambitious mother had arranged for her to model clothes for Sears catalogues. She worked for years until a buxom adolescence put an end to her career. Lilly went to college, hoping to major in fashion design, but her mother forbade it, insisting she study merchandising instead. After graduation, Lilly went to work in a department store selling lingerie. At nights she modeled, rebelliously without clothes, for a group of amateur artists. She met my father, a Sunday painter. They married and she left her mother's house, leaving behind the framed tearsheets of Lilly's beautifully catalogued life. Lilly curtsying in crinolines, Lilly saluting in sailor denim set with sailor hat, Lilly in white lace and tiara, drinking tea from a tea set, $14.99.

My mother always understood beauty, in the way that beautiful people do. She saw how people liked to be around it and instinctively understood its place in the world of important things. Through my father, Lilly discovered that beauty also came in nice square canvases bearing images and messages. For Lilly, the door opened, the bell rang. Through association with art she could have feelings, success, control. She expressed herself through her collection. She defined beauty instead of it defining her. With Lilly as the driving force, my parents bought low and sold high. She kept her job at Macy's and sold underwear, for art's sake, until she could afford not to; a businesswoman for the sake of a greater cause. Like Wally, art was her religion.

In fact, my paintings embarrassed Lilly. Even though work like mine was highly saleable and never went out of style, it didn't fit the niche she had hoped to carve for me and meant a lifetime of less discerning clients and less important galleries.

"The eye is all-important," Lilly liked to say. I had found that to be her best advice. Most people, I had discovered, only glanced, did not choose to look at things closely. At Jenks and Wolenska, it was not my knowledge of food that brought me quick promotions but my trained eye for detail. I had risen from the ranks of stockroom clerk, shelving clerk, cookbook clerk and was on my way to becoming one of J&W's best linguine experts. That day, I was routinely wiping down the marble counter under the crock of cornichons when I discovered a small leak in the ceramic. I was about to get Ms. Jenks when suddenly I saw my mother standing in front of me.

Lilly was a tall, buxom woman with rich black hair coiled around her head like a crown. She had a square, jutting jaw and carried herself like a diva. Her size embarrassed her, as though it belied the aesthetics that had ruled her life. Never an ornate woman, rather a carefully designed one, she built herself to scale every morning before she left for work. Like a building, every brick was arranged. Lilly was a piece of work.

She had not spoken to me since I had left art school. I had missed her, and I could see that despite herself she had missed me. She stood there like royalty as she offered her cheek as a peace offering. There had been no point asking to see her until she was ready to see me. I was glad to lean forward and give a kiss. She looked from right to left into the long store piled high with delicacies.

"Ridiculous," she said. "To throw away a talent like yours for *this*. I suppose you mean to continue carrying on this way?"

I let her do all the talking, it would be over faster that way. I gave the marble top another wipe.

"I should have sent you to law school or insisted you be a doctor. You might have valued your talent if you had to struggle for it. I made it too easy."

The briny green juice formed a larger ring around the bottom of the crock. I wiped a little faster.

She watched me, her eyes wet. "Those hands." There was love in her voice, not for me exactly, but close. She took another one-hundred-and-eighty-degree look around at the store. "The waste." She shook her head.

I tried to get the attention of another clerk who was staring at my mother. *Get Jenks*, I mouthed. I mopped a little faster. The juice was spreading rapidly over the marble. Was there a cosmic message here?

"I hate to interrupt, Mother, but I think we have a little problem here." I had to get to Ms. Jenks, I just had to. The crock was leaking at a rate faster than I could wipe, the cornichons showing their dark little heads through the crack.

"Problem," my mother snorted. "I'd call it a crisis."

Indeed it was, as a flood of minuscule pickles began to pour out over the marble counter faster than I could mop.

"Step back, please," the unmistakably authoritarian voice of

Jenks announced as she arrived with two young male rescuers in tow. One lifted the crock, the other held a rubber basin below it, and off they carried the patient to the basement to recover in the company of other ailing crocks.

My mother looked disapprovingly at the stalky Jenks. I understood now: Lilly had come to rescue me.

"If you *must* have this, Kitchie," she said wearily, "you must have *better* than this."

I thought, *What could be better than this?* We were at the very pinnacle of the food world, a veritable Museum of Modern Food. I began to doubt my mother's sensibility.

"I know a man," she said solemnly, "*of great artistic integrity.* . . . "

And so I came to work for the Baron Bernard DeGroat. My mother had bought a Bellows from his private collection, a small study for one of his larger works. The chance to work for someone of such stature as the Baron came once in a lifetime. Even Ms. Jenks said it was a golden opportunity as she handed me my last Jenks and Wolenska paycheck and wished me well. The Baron was famous for two classic volumes, one about a sweet amber liquor made by monks, the other about an innkeeper's life in Provence.

The Baron lived with his wife in a large, rambling Upper East Side apartment filled with worn oriental rugs and a curious mix of old English mahogany and modernist Deco furniture. His British wife, Eveline, who had first let me in the door, was barely four feet tall. She wore her gray hair in a bun that hung lopsided on her head, held there by two yellow pencils.

"I'm *so* glad you're here," she said with fluttering gratitude.

She showed me into a large living area lined with bookcases filled with cookbooks. There the Baron sat in a large armchair just right for his ample frame. He was a large, puffy man with a huge bald head. The Baron wore needlepoint slippers on his swollen feet, and by his side was Claire, his Seeing Eye dog. The Baron rubbed Claire's overfed belly and appeared to look me up and down as I entered the room. His eyes were not distorted by his blindness, and he wore no sunglasses, giving him the illusion of a blind man who could see. In fact, very few of the Baron's fans knew he was blind.

The Baron had suffered a wound to his head during the Second World War. There was irreparable damage to his eyes, and he gradually lost his vision. Since the young Bernard had worked as a journalist before the war, he knew he could write, especially about the finer things in life, which he considered to be art, food and wine.

"A blind man cannot write about art, and even if he could, who would believe him?" He shook his head. "But food?" He wagged a large index finger at me. "Everyone knows that the blind have extraordinary powers of taste," he sniggered. Was he sneering at the cliché, or did he resent that his tongue was his only means to a living?

I was to be the Baron's eyes, to take up where Claire left off.

"She can't do everything," he explained wistfully. I had the impression he wished she could. He couldn't be easy on people, I thought. Much more tolerant of dogs.

My job involved cooking in his test kitchen, trying out recipes, and testing new kitchen gadgets. I also read the mail and newly published cookbooks out loud to him, arranged and updated his recipe files, and helped him write his articles on food and travel, his cookbook in progress, *History of the Casserole*, and his soon-to-be-published magnus opus, *Miel*, about a beekeeper he knew in Alsace during the war. I was an extension of his body, hired hands, good for jotting down whatever he didn't note on the tape recorder. I would read to him from his typed manuscript while he sat large and impassive, his long chunky legs sprawled out, his forefinger pressed deep into his mushy cheek, as though engrossed in some internal movie. The secret of the Baron's success was that writing about food gave him back his sight.

That and the fact that he drove whoever worked for him crazy. He could hear a mistake from across the room. He who had overcome life's injustice had no pity for the rest of us. We were to hang up our shortcomings on a hook by the door when we entered his kitchen. He would tolerate no mistakes as we julienned carrots and celery. Eveline, who always looked whipped and disheveled, more often than not had already been crying by the time I arrived in the mornings. We worked side by side in the kitchen but he found special fault with his wife's mincing and chopping. "Shall I throw it in the garbage, then, *dear*?" she would ask disingenuously.

Copper was his pride and passion. When we weren't busy, we shined the Baron's copper pots. He touched them with the same tenderness with which he petted his dog's chest.

The most important part of my job was to accompany the Baron to and from his weekly segment as food reporter on a morning television show, *Wake Up, America*. The Baron's spot was called *Eat Up, America*. He filled his five minutes with reports on everything from new kitchen inventions to recipes for elegant hors d'oeuvres, quick dinners, complicated desserts. Sometimes he ran contests for the best pancakes or the best fudge sauce.

He wanted me to handle him so that he would never appear blind. This dubious proposition made me dread our weekly trips to the television station. As his Seeing Eye human, I was to hold him by the left arm as though he were holding me. A tap on his arm meant stop, two taps, step up, three, step down. If an executive of the TV station were approaching, I was to pinch him gently and give the name of the oncomer in a discreet way, careful not to move my lips too much. My job depended on grace, manners and parlor-trick ventriloquy.

The morning I lost my job with the Baron, I'd overslept. The Baron's chauffeur, Jerry, rang my buzzer until I leapt out of bed, opened the window, and yelled down that I'd be right there. I pulled on my clothes and, since I couldn't find the right shoes, wore a pair of flats I'd meant to take to the shoemaker to glue the sole. I ran down the stairs, the loose flap of my shoe plopping alongside me. Jerry looked uncomfortably at his watch, door ready and open. As we sped uptown to pick up Baron De-Groat, Jerry and I discussed the merits of Emerson clock radios versus Big Ben windups for $7.95, available at any drugstore.

Eveline DeGroat was already in the lobby standing next to her sulking husband. She looked like a butterfly this morning. She'd tied her wispy gray hair away from her face with a little blue piece of satin, and the bow had come undone, giving the defeated impression of limp antennae. Like a captured butterfly, her kimono sleeves hung like wings.

"Here's for you, then," Eveline said, handing over the Baron to me. I imagined her spending her morning in his favorite armchair, smoking Gauloises, stubbing out the butts in his favorite copper bowl.

Once inside the limo, the Baron launched a combat attack on

my tardiness, cruised into high-gear disappointment at my lack of professionalism, plummeted to despair at my hopeless youth and inexperience, and, as we pulled up the station, swerved to a crash landing known as my *last chance.*

As I walked shakily through the lobby of the television studio, my heel flapped along the marble floor.

The Baron stood still.

"What *is* that disgusting sound?" he asked.

He couldn't walk without me, but I was the one who felt useless and expendable.

The television studio was large, dark, filled with the cameras and props that turn illusion into tube reality. The hosts' backdrop was a big yellow sun radiating orange spokes behind two blue mountainous shapes, a logo meant to convey morning bursting forth all over the land, as in, *Wake Up, America.* To the left was the Baron's set, a gleaming mock kitchen with cabinets, copper pots, hanging plants and a windowed door looking out onto a field composed of the same *Wake Up* landscape that married country and city.

I delivered the Baron first to Makeup where he was powdered and combed. Wardrobe gave him a gold brocade vest to wear under his apron, with matching gold bow tie. When they were satisfied they sent him off clothed, rouged, and free of nose shine into the world of rating wars. Though he looked distinguished, neither Makeup nor Wardrobe could pump animation into the Baron's lumberous body. Evan, his young producer, led us to the set where the morning took on a bitter taste.

"Now I know how you're going to feel about this, Bernie, and believe me I understand, but, Bernie, there are things that happen on live performance that, well, let me cut to the chase and I'm sorry I have to be the one to say it, Bernie, but all the copper pots on your set have been replaced."

The Baron stood motionless on the set, orange spokes of sun bursting out cheerfully behind him.

"Not replaced, exactly," Evan continued, "more like stolen."

"Stolen?" The Baron was enraged. "By whom?"

Evan muttered under his breath. "Actually, we think it was one of the crew. Prop guy who loves cooking and his wife have a big copper collection in their own kitchen. Lives in Hempstead," he explained. "But it's so circumstantial, it might as well be hearsay." He stepped in closer to our faces and confided further, "What should I do, ask him if he's a thief?" He shook his head at the sheer madness of such a thought. "With the unions the way they are today, nuh-uh-uh."

"But I can't possibly whisk in these—" The Baron fingered a set of bowls placed before him on the set.

"Just for today, Bernie. These are *real* stainless steel, sprayed with copper paint on the outside so that the camera picks up copper, *reads* copper. I think, if you could see them, you'd agree we've done a fine job." Evan smiled at me and winked.

"What do you think, Kitch? It works, right? Here, take a look at it on the camera," Evan invited me.

"Baron?" I asked.

"Oh, go on," he said, wearily leaning on the beige Formica counter between the set's cook top and sink.

I looked into the camera's eyepiece and had to admit I saw absolutely no difference between real copper and sprayed copper. I returned to the Baron, who was now submitting to lighting tests.

"But Evan, couldn't you possibly *buy* some pots before we go on?" the Baron whined.

Evan shook his head. Was he dealing with a baby here or what?

"Bernie, Bernie, it's six o'clock in the morning. Who's gonna sell you copper pots? I tried to pick up a roll and coffee this morning on my way to work. Know how hard *that* is at six A.M., Bernie?"

"It doesn't look so bad, it really doesn't," I reassured the Baron.

He hated reassurance when what he wanted was agreement. "You wouldn't know real copper from spray paint if your life depended on it."

Evan slunk away from the set and left me to fend for myself.

Wake Up, America would start in ten minutes, and we still hadn't rehearsed all the movements around the kitchen, the body language of cooking. We worked with a kind of kinesic script which read like a description of the cha-cha or the merengue. We began with the intro, the set-up shot, the shot, then moved into the pantomime of cooking while I guided his hands over pots, pans, whisks, bowls, measuring cups, wooden spoons. It was the same kind of box step that I taught him every week. *Three steps front, two steps left, four steps right. Sink to counter, oven to stove, pot to bowl. Walk two steps left, open wall oven, three steps back to butcher block, two steps left to the sink, and four steps forward to the chopping board.*

Because the script called for so many appliances that morning, the set swarmed with wires. It was like standing on a bed of snakes. One set of wires was caught in my shoe, sandwiched between my leather uppers and my loose sole.

. . . after the roast is lifted out of the oven, Baron, it's three steps back to the chopping board, knife is two inches from the roast, stool is

to your left, slice roast on serving platter for close-up shot, take fork in left hand, point back left to oven, hold platter up to face, sniff, smile, turn right, four feet back to wooden island, rest right hand on bowl of roast potatoes —

"You read me that line already, imbecile."

The wires on the set had wound around my feet again. As I disentangled more cable from my loose sole, I reminded myself to be careful not to fall. An accident could cost me my job with the Baron.

I tried to concentrate on leading him through the script, guiding his hands and moving him from the sink-counter area back to the stove-oven area. As I guided his hands from the whisk over to the painted copper bowls, his hands got to the bowls before mine did. Before I could lift my hands off the bowl, his fingers discovered mine. The morning had proved too much for the old perfectionist, and he whacked at my hands like an acerbic game of Slaphappy. Typically, he hadn't any sense of his body's size or strength and the force of his swats threw me completely off balance. My feet gave way. I fell backwards and tried to regain my balance, but the loose sole of my shoe ate wire cable one last time. As I took the fall, I watched him topple over too.

Nothing is worse than watching a big blind man fall, unless he is falling on you. First his mike flew off, then the buttons popped off his gold brocade vest. His arms swam in the air and, when he crashed on top of me, the weight of his body fell like a heavy oak across my knee. I felt a cracking, burning sensation, but this was quickly forgotten as some of the flimsier setups and props now fell on us. Bowls, dishes, platters, carving fork and knife followed. Kitchenware was spread out around us like a picnic gone awry.

The Baron didn't have to fire me. I knew right then and there, tangled up together like fallen trees after a hurricane, that this was the end of my career assisting a great food writer and television personality. It was destiny. I was meant for other work.

The blind gourmet's segment was hastily canceled for that morning. After the crew untangled us, the Baron was so furious that Evan thought it best to separate us. Jerry took me to an emergency room where I turned out to have a dislocated kneecap. Evan took the Baron home by taxi.

At home, I slept. I woke up, ate oatmeal, and found it almost as reassuring as painkillers. So much for men of great artistic integrity and jobs obtained through family sources. Chemically speaking, some people should never work together. Frankly, I was glad not to be the Baron's eyes anymore. After me, the Baron hired a ballet student, and I heard through Jerry, who brought me groceries until I was well enough to climb stairs again, that the arrangement proved very successful.

The Baron and Evan must have worked out that copper pot problem because when I watched him the next Thursday morning on television, leg propped up, resting on my bed, I could see that all the copper pots on the set were gleaming, and they really looked *real*, just the way the Baron liked them. At least I thought they were real. I mean, they looked that way to me then. I know if I saw them now, I'd be able to tell the difference, for sure.

Three

I holed up in my apartment all of April while my knee healed. I now understood the inherent flaw to employment; a person could get fired. I wanted to cook for a living, but I didn't want to feel expendable. Like a jailbird, I stared wistfully at the courtyard trees sprouting their little buds. If nature could break through concrete, I could be my own boss. It was springtime, anything was possible.

I missed fresh air the way you miss a thing when you can't have it. I wasn't having a lot of things then. A boyfriend, for one. What I didn't know about love could have filled a bottomless punch bowl. I had grown up with collectors who worshiped artists. Naturally, that is what I expected for myself. My ideal lover would be someone who would devote himself to my budding, if as yet unformed, food career. Clearly, it wasn't the frenzy of new love and its manic passions I wanted as much as a promoter. Was I in the market for a lover or an agent? I was used to the idea of people paying homage to talent. My parents had built their reputation and a small fortune on their devotion to painters. Should I have wanted anything less for myself just because my metier was food?

My best friend Ginger visited me every day. She brought

flowers, groceries and cookbooks from the library. Ginger had that rare quality, availability. She was a genius at taking care of other people. Ginger had red hair, pale skin that freckled in the summer and a generous, reliable body. For three generations, the women in her family had been social workers. Ginger was bred to the cause, but every time the subject of social work school came up, she balked. She had a strong sense of what other people's lives needed and could size up human problems like the Queen of Situations. She was far less accurate when it came to her own life. The last time she had put off social work school, it was to help her husband save his failing carpentry business. She was probably on the verge of admitting she couldn't help Steve salvage his carpentry shop when, in the nick of time, my problems distracted her. Otherwise, Ginger might have noticed that her marriage was crumbling.

One afternoon during my convalescence, Ginger brought me a bag of zepoles, hot, greasy blobs of yeasty deep-fried dough powdered with confectioners' sugar.

"Where'd you get these?" I asked, licking my fingers.

"Street fair," she said in between her own bites, "Upper West Side. They're all over these days. A new one pops up every weekend in someone else's neighborhood. I almost brought you a sausage-pepper thing, but somehow this greasy dough seemed more curative."

I licked the powdered sugar off my fingers. "My knee feels better already."

"You know, maybe Stevie should sell his stuff at one of these street things. I've been encouraging him to work on this new yo-yo idea of his. Can I use your phone? I want to see how he is, he's been so depressed lately. What do you think?"

"Yo-yos sound good to me."

While Ginger checked up on her other patient, I finished off the last medicinal blob of fried dough.

As soon as my knee had healed, I took the advice Ginger gave her husband and started to sell sandwiches at street fairs. I celebrated with the Arabs of Staten Island, cried with the Jews of Williamsburg, carnivaled with the Caribbeans of Flatbush Avenue, ristaffeled with the Indonesians in Queens, paprikashed till I was red in the face in little Hungary. I even helped Ninth Avenue celebrate itself.

I catered the streets: *Be A Wandering Gourmet. Eat While You Walk. Great Sandwiches from Kitchie's Kitchen.* Naturally, I anguished long and hard over the right sandwich combinations: liverwurst and Muenster with Creole mustard, cream cheese and pistachios on raisin pumpernickel, homemade pork terrine and sauerkraut on rye.

One fair started out just like the next, and the Atlantic Antic was no exception. The blue sky promised a day of beautiful weather. The Brooklyn streets were calm, traffic had not yet reached its urban pitch. Vendors arrived at 7:00 A.M. with bundles, boxes and folding tables. They counted up the change in their banks, emptied boxes of sellables onto the tables: antiques, costume jewelry, batik bikinis, items of every imaginable use and no possible use at all.

Most of the vendors were weekend amateurs. Families trying to make a few bucks, a few people like myself trying to start up a small business. Old-timers, who made their living by street work, had faces that were lined and weathered by the outdoors. Like entrepreneurial gypsies, their caravan business life was a point of pride. They remembered the towns where they'd done well and what they'd sold there: underwear in Wichita, kitchen towels and hot mitts in Schenectady. The old-timers traded stories about fairgrounds, boarding houses and tornadoes. A few were bitter: trust in God, all others pay cash, and don't let kids touch the goods. Sometimes this life seemed about as much fun as a Diane Arbus festival, but for the most part, I enjoyed myself that summer.

I had quickly learned the ropes: arrive early; bring a hundred dollars in change, a book to kill time, suntan lotion SPF#30, a thermos of hot or cold coffee; and make friends with the next table in case you have to use the Portasan. I was one of the regulars working the city circuit. I waved hello to the young children who insisted on wearing their parents' change aprons. I joked confidently with the old-timers who would be traveling south after Thanksgiving. I could go with them and travel like a gypsy until I found a perfect small town where I would want to settle down, enjoy the climate, rent a little storefront, maybe a luncheonette, turn it into a classy little spot where I would serve great granola, whole grain waffles, cassoulets and navarins and, in time, my own wine list. . . .

I had gotten as far as Key West when I noticed *him* watching me. He sat across the street and down a few tables. I'd seen him before. He had worked as many fairs as I had. He had been watching me all morning, and whenever I looked up he wouldn't look away. He had an all-American face: blue eyes, blond hair, strong cheekbones, a football hero who came from generations of mayors and aldermen, deacons and judges, with front porch manners, used to plenty of elderberry pies and clandestine moonshine. The regular stared at me all afternoon. He looked to be the same age as me. His long, blond, corkscrew curls spilled rebelliously over his forehead.

He leaned way back on two legs of his chair with his feet up on his table. He dangled a cigar from his mouth, a wise guy. Self-reliant. Definite lumberjack material. *Timber.* You could get out of his way or not; he'd never consider your broken leg his problem. Motorcyclist tendencies, with a streak of Hell's Angels running right through him.

So what was it he sold, pictures? He had hung them behind him like a curtain or backdrop and in the sun they seemed to flicker. Optical illusion, I told myself. He watched as I squinted at the simple pictures that at first looked like children's book illustrations: *sun setting over snowy mountaintop, moon shimmering over lake, geese flying over autumnal wheat field, sailboats set on sunlit seas, faithful dog sleeping by a fiery hearth.* Currier and Ives knock-offs, printed on metallic paper so that the silvery streams and gleaming snows glistened and glittered. How could such a beautiful man sell an item as tasteless as a 3-D Jesus winking his eye on top of next year's calendar?

I spent the rest of the day trying to avoid his eyes, but every time I looked up he was there. He sat watching every move I made from under the flinty shade of his cowboy hat. He leaned as far back as gravity would allow, inviting trouble. That whole afternoon I watched him watch me some more. From time to time I would look up and catch his eyes, but he never looked away. I could feel the heat spread across my cheeks, my fingers grow clumsy, my body weighed down by a different kind of hunger; a desire as fancy as one of his silvery pictures. His stare drilled into my skin. My lips felt heavy. I bit them. I needed a drink. Everything on me needed watering. All of me was scratchy and dry. Not that I wanted him to stop. The longer he stared, the better I felt. Every time I caught his eyes, he was there. Until, finally, at the end of the afternoon, he *was* there.

He stood in front of my table surveying my sandwiches, smiling, his eyes the color of blue ice. Was he studied or authentic? Polo or White Trash? His nails were dirty, his knuckles were stained, his shoes looked like they had seen plaster and mud. He had that certain smell, eau d'automobile, the sweet muskiness of a dirty three-year-old who has played all afternoon in a city park, a certain coming together of the odors that tell of the male proclivity for poking, pushing and fixing.

"Hey, you have egg salad sangweech?"

My ears needed cleaning. The Marlboro Man had opened his mouth and the Cyrillic alphabet fell out. Hard to place the accent. An undertone of Slavic warmth?

"No, eh?" he answered for me. He seemed genuinely disappointed. "I am sorry," he explained, "eggs is my favorite flavor."

He picked up a pâté sandwich, impressed.

"Three bucks. Hey, some good price you getting over here." He unwrapped the package dexterously. He was good with his hands. "You got ketchup? I like." He bit into it. "Delicioso." He winked at me and smiled. "Scrumpshoos, eh?"

Did his tendency to drop articles make him more or less appealing? I couldn't decide. By now, any thought of him as a southern fullback had gone with the wind, and the residual picture of him on a veranda just made me smile.

He smiled back.

"Is very excellent sangweech," he complimented me, talking with his mouth full. "But next time you gonna bring ketchup for me, right? Then I gonna *love* you sangweech like *crazy*."

He continued to chew standing in front of me. What was it that made people want to eat near me all the time? I watched the lines of his jaw move up and down. He was sinewy. Of all the models I'd sketched, none was as inspiring as this face and body. The space between us was thick and heady. He ate, and I watched.

"I think sangweech most sexy food." He spoke philosophically, mouth full, looking into my eyes, never looking away. "Feeling most important part."

"Feeling?"

He looked at me like I was crazy. He held out the half-eaten sandwich. "Sure. Middle of sangweech is *feeling*."

I clammed.

"Cat got you tongue?" he asked between two ravenous bites. He ate as though this was his first meal in days, it was hunger sans politesse. No apologies, here was a man whose appetite was unappeasable.

He picked another sandwich, held it up to me to show me. Ratatouille and mozzarella. I wondered if he was going to pay me and if it mattered if he didn't. Where did this guy come from, and didn't they ever feed him there? He stood to the side chewing some more, while I made change for other customers, two talky women who asked me for a recipe. I had a hard time remembering the recipe, let alone telling them, while he watched me. After they left he stood thoughtfully sipping a bottle of orange soda.

"Why you so shy with those nice peoples? They not gonna bite you."

Though his tone was very assertive and clipped, he didn't mean to be unkind. He wanted to give me advice, this Dale Carnegie of the streets. He wiped the soda mustache from his lips.

"They like you, they like you food, they wonder how you do this magic. They eat, they want little piece of you, like souvenir. So why you don't shake some conversation out?"

"I—I couldn't think of anything to say."

"Lessen, you got plenty to say. I tell you what you gonna do. Stick to cooking, food. Stick to basic stuff, their kids, their job. Is summer, ask them where they going on vacation. You gonna have no problem, believe me."

I believed him.

He wiped his mouth coarsely with a napkin, crumpled it and the sandwich wrapper into a ball, and tossed it into the garbage can by his feet. He cleared his throat, as if to make room for the next item on the agenda. He clapped his hands together and rubbed them as if warming himself in front of my fire.

"So, you got more kinds sangweeches I haven't tried yet?"

It was hard to concentrate with sexual heat wrapping my body like a fango mudpack.

"Tuna with capers and dried apricots, fresh sardine and cheddar on seven grain with mustard dressing, and chicken salad with almond butter and young spring lettuce." I caught my breath. "On semolina," I smiled weakly.

"Sardine-Cheeder, whatta hell." Then he took out of his pocket not a wallet, but a wad of singles. He handed me enough to pay for his entire lunch, and said, "Is good to try new things, no?" He peeled the saran wrap off the sandwich and took another savage bite. Bite *me*, I thought. He chewed, his taut jaw full of sandwich as though he wanted me to watch him chew. I obliged. I never took my eyes off him, off his beautiful lips. I was like a stove turned on high in a summer kitchen.

Another customer came and bought a chicken salad and I

fumbled while making change and spilled the entire cash box. Coins and dollar bills fell under the table. I grew red and picked up my change from the ground. If he had only stood there and watched me from the side as I bent down, perhaps it would have been all over. His inattentiveness might have served like a pitcher of cold water splashed across my face—I would have come to. But no, he bent down on the other side of the table and gathered coins, meeting me under the folding table, arranging them in long columns before he handed them to me or put them in my cash box. He put one long column of quarters in my hand, closed my fingers over it, and held it there. He smelled of sardines when he spoke, my sardines. "Don't drop what I am giving you, now," he warned me softly.

He ate four of my sandwiches that afternoon. At the end of the day, I felt obliged to buy a Silver Fantasy from him. I chose a picture of a lake and a little thatched cabin with smoke curling out of its chimney. The kind of place I hoped I might live in one day.

At the end of the day the street fair had a haggard, tattered quality. Streets cluttered with people gave way to littered gutters and overflowing garbage cans. The avenue looked tired and spent. I started packing up when, suddenly, he was standing in front of me again, a cigar dangling out of his mouth, unlit this time, carrying his boxes behind him.

"Hey, I'm gonna help you fold you tables."

He took charge of the breakdown while I cleaned up, painfully aware of my flushed cheeks.

"You know, we in Brooklyn now," he said when we were done. R's rolled off his tongue like water over rocks in a shallow stream. Of course I knew we were in Brooklyn.

"Is excellent place for Middle Eastern food."

Ah.

"I know little Lebanese place, few blocks down Court Street."

We wheeled our boxes through downtown Brooklyn in the twilight. His name was Gunnar, he had been brought up in Finland by his mother, his father was Russian. He had earned a B.A. at City College in engineering, but he was more interested in business. He was not surprised that I had studied art. "You look it," he said. "But leesen," he abruptly changed the subject as we stood in front of a liquor store stopping to buy wine for dinner, "important thing is, do you have boyfriend?" After I assured him I had none, he cheerfully chose two bottles of Chardonnay instead of one, to go with dinner.

He brought us to a restaurant whose name seemed to be It Pays To Eat Well. The dining room was decorated with hanging glass that cast shadows in primary colors around the room. The walls were hung with cheap, dark tapestries. We sat at a corner table eating from the land of yogurt, eggplant and tahini.

"You like baba ganoush?" he asked, ordering for both of us.

All night the smell of pomegranates, honey and mint hung over our heads. The baba ganoush was as lavish as love as we scooped the spread and ate it off torn pita. The wine loosened us and we laughed, and I knew then that we could get along.

I took food from his plate and looked into his eyes as he emptied his glass of wine and touched his hand as he poured another. Our conversation was harsh compared to the language of love that was our dinner.

"So, Gunnar, you like working street fairs?" I expected to compare notes on the old-timers and talk about Key West in

November. But Gunnar never said anything I expected him to say.

"Street fairs? They are okay. More, I prefer to work indoors. Also, I like nighttime. Is not my preference to work day. I am, how you say, owl. But I tell myself, 'Why not?' If you want to make money, you have to start somewheres."

"How did you come to sell those, uh—."

"Silver Fantasies?" He smiled proudly. He was glad I had brought the subject up.

"First time I see them I know people gonna like them. I don't even know if they ugly or what, but right away I know people gonna buy. Moroccan guy in Provincetown give me sole right to concession for all five boroughs in city." He banged his chest emphatically. "I am sole representative of Silver Fantasies, New York. Is good opportunity, no?" He pulled a cigar from his shirt pocket, sucked as he held a match to it, and looked at it thoughtfully as he held it between thumb and forefinger. "Special revolutionary printing process. Is shit, I know, but you can't help to like, right? Sure." He happily answered his own question. "Everybody loves," he said philosophically. "Is good fantasy. Cheap for price, eh?" he mused and blew two perfect smoke rings.

"Hey, this smoke is bothering you? Tell me."

It was, but I didn't.

"So, you are cooking lady? You want restaurant?"

"Well, maybe. I mean, a small one, yes. Somewhere warm, by the water maybe. Just a few tables, no more than twenty customers a night. Small menu, very personal, but listen to me going on, and I only just started selling sandwiches—"

He rescued me.

"Leesen, Keetchie, everybody in this country wants something. That is why I am here too."

The rest of dinner was filled with his ideas, his opinions. Mostly, I listened.

"Doesn't matter what you sell. Just has to make money. I am needing money to live, so just I am selling these things." He studied me. "You don't like very much, hmm? You think it makes less of me, what I sell?" He stopped to consider this possibility, watching his smoke dissipate into the air. He smiled. "Maybe, maybe not. Is free country."

I considered what I had here. Aggressive, college-educated foreigner with street smarts. Capitalism coursing through his veins like testosterone. He was more American than cherry pie.

Gunnar paid the bill, in cash that bulged in the left pocket of his pants.

"Come on," he said, taking charge, "I take you home." It occurred to me later in the taxi as we whizzed across the Brooklyn Bridge into Manhattan that I didn't know whether he meant my home or his. Not knowing what Gunnar meant was part of his appeal.

Four

His apartment turned out to be on the same street as mine, only several avenues deeper into the heart of the alphabet. His tenement was on Seventh between C and D. No lock on the front door. It swung wide open like a democracy, letting anyone in. The hallway was dimly lit. Even this late at night I heard televisions blasting, radios blaring, kids whining, and mothers screaming. It was that Lower East Side monster, the building that never sleeps. Gunnar lived on the first floor. Before he took out his keys, he banged on the door and rattled the doorknob, adding to the hallway din significantly.

"Hey!" he yelled, "I'm home, you bastards, last chance, get out! Is *my* turn now to use apartment."

He might have been warning roommates.

He turned to me and smiled politely. "Everyone deserves proper warning, don't you think? Even thief. This way, thief leaves before I walk in. I am alive. Everybody has what they want, everybody is happy."

"Have you ever been broken into?"

"No, but why take chance?" He turned the key in the cylinder. "I got valuable collections in here, besides, I am with you. I don't want to risk."

The lights were already on. I supposed he never turned them off, another warning for intruders. Gunnar's apartment was one large room. There was a Truffaut movie poster in the kitchen area and several plants on the windowsill—a good sign; he was able to keep living things alive. He wasn't big on house-cleaning; the dust and hairballs collected under his bed like tumbleweed. His taste ran to the exotic. His bedspread was African, his table was hand-carved from Mexico, his curtains, hand-blocked batik. On the top of an antique desk, its missing leg replaced by a pile of used college texts, were several card-board boxes filled with Gunnar's Silver Fantasies.

Two shelves ran the length of the wall displaying collections from an American childhood he'd never had: jars of marbles, toy guns, including an old ivory-handled Hopalong Cassidy, dozens of Pez dispensers, each with a different cartoon charac-ter head, a pile of old Marvel comics, and hundreds of political buttons from past elections: I like Ike.

"So, this is my home life," he said by way of welcoming me to his apartment. "You like share?" Was he offering me a chair or asking me to move in with him? We'd spent the earlier part of the evening in a bed of baba ganoush, so anything was possible. There was no way of knowing what he meant, and I couldn't think of anything to say. I sat down. Let him figure it out, I thought. Let him do the talking.

The lovemaking was very tender. He was a generous lover. He pleased himself by pleasing me. He didn't need to be touched or caressed, he was only interested in winning me, and he did, over and over. I felt like a cat warming to his body. If I gave him a shoulder, he rubbed it; if I showed him my neck, he kissed it. He seemed only to want to satisfy me, and he did. His body was lean, muscular. My soft flesh must have felt like a pillow to him. I was hungry for this lovemaking, but he was starving. He made me feel that I was filling him.

Whatever sex I had had before, it had never been like this. Did we have something special or did he enjoy sex like this every night? Once a week? Once a month? I spent a few minutes trying to imagine his sexual calendar, then gave up. We lay there, the nighttime breeze covering us.

"Tell me about yourself," I said, stroking his chest.

He was quiet for a long time, then reached behind him and propped the pillows under his head and sighed. The spell was broken.

"Long story. Covers two continents," he warned me. He smiled vulnerably as he looked at me, wondering whether to move towards me or away.

"My father worked in marine station," he struggled for his words, "oceanographic institute. He was biologist in Murmansk near Finnish border. He traveled across border always collecting samples. He met my mother up north at Lake Inari, near Lap country. She was secretary on vacation, he spoke her language, they married, I was born. I am Finnish national. They stopped to get along, so he stopped to come across border so much. Most times I live with her in Rovaniemi where she was typist. Other times I live with him at station, and sometimes we visit Leningrad together. When I was teenager my father got chance to come to this country on exchange; marine station there, very big, very famous. He got visa to work for aquarium in Coney Island, so I come with him. I learn English, work hard, get through college." He started to laugh, "Life, hmm? From Lapland to Brooklyn."

Gunnar spent his adolescence on the Boardwalk, making money in the summers taking Polaroids of sunbathers who wanted to remember their day at Coney Island.

"Always I was selling something," he said, "or going to school. My father was all time busy at work, I was left on my own to grow up rest of way, American. Gambling, that's what my father and I did together on weekends." They played the horses, the dogs, roosters; they played anything that promised more return on their money than a bank.

"Not exactly 'Leave It To Beaver' Finnish-Ugric style," I said.

"Hey, I am good citizen now," he said earnestly. "I pay taxes."

I stroked his neck, his shoulders. His firm body brought to mind anatomy textbooks with their diagrams and colored plates of muscles exposed under splayed skin, tendons long and taut like strands of power that lay in wait to move, to throw, to make, to build. As I fell asleep it seemed to me that this body would have no trouble taking me wherever I wanted to go.

In the morning we had coffee and some stale glazed donuts. He had to go to Provincetown to pick up more Silver Fantasies and settle some business there with the distributor. He didn't like doing business over the phones and didn't trust the mail. His car would get us there quickly, would I like to come? I had nothing pressing. I wasn't painting for deadlines anymore, and the next fair wasn't until the weekend, so I said yes. His car turned out to be a black Austin Healey convertible. He parked it on the street. I ran my hand along its sleek shiny side.

"So, Gunnar, the Silver Fantasy business is good?"

He looked at me sheepishly. He adjusted his Chicago Cubs baseball hat and turned to me seriously, conspiratorially.

"You are only one I am telling, but is stolen car, I think. I buy it from some guy on Fifth Street, next to police station. Runs pretty good, anyway." He was a man of contradictions, so what did one more matter?

We set off with the top down. It was early, and the streets were empty. The breeze felt good, my hair swirled around my face. As we picked up speed, he reached into his glove compartment and removed a red silk scarf.

"Maybe you will need to use for hair?" he offered innocently.

I wondered how many other women had gotten the red scarf in the speeding sports car treatment.

"Is only polite to offer, no?" he asked, somewhat confused by my obvious irritation.

Gunnar drove me home and parked outside while I ran upstairs and packed a small bag. Toothbrush, hairbrush, jeans, shirts; I thought I had everything. I turned out the light, locked up, then let myself in again. I went to my dresser and out of the top right drawer I grabbed one of my own head scarves before locking up once again and joining him in the car. Off we went, speeding towards Provincetown. The air sweetened once we left the city, and once we hit the Cape, the drive was full of piney woods, scrub and sand racing alongside the road.

Provincetown held a special set of associations for me. By the time I was twelve, my parents were dealing full time and making good money. A few years before my father died, and every year thereafter, we vacationed there. Once a community of Portuguese fishermen on the northern tip of Cape Cod, the town had sprouted theaters, galleries, museums, bookstores, two natural food restaurants and a growing homosexual community. A tourist mecca, its main street was jammed with stores offering the newest and most preposterous in souvenirs and T-shirts of the sort that haunt all summer tinsel towns.

An unlikely place for Lilly and Theo to have spent summer vacations but for the fact that for many decades the town had been an artists' colony. Summer was the only time of year my parents expressed any interest in contemporary art. I suspect they were more interested in the artists themselves than in their work, of which they bought little. They enjoyed the social life that belonged to this small summer community. They visited old friends' studios and galleries, carried on about the Huntington Hartford Museum, attended parties and readings, wore unconventional dress, drank tequila punches, ate Portuguese sausages, sported their vacation personae.

Every summer, we'd rent the same cottage in the dunes, with its quaint furniture and wall posters. The first thing Lilly and Theo did was remove any posters to cleanse the house of bad art. Then they went to the A&P, stocked up on frozen staples, made the beds, and began their version of relaxing. Lilly let loose with the pedal pushers and hit the beach protected by her wide-brimmed straw hat. My father sat under the umbrella with her, absorbed in a spy novel, all he ever read, the one genre, he claimed, that helped him formulate better art deals.

Late afternoons and evenings were filled with vodka martinis and cigarettes at the Motherwells', violin concerts at Chaim Gross' high on the hill, sunsets and readings at the Mailers', and at the Byron Brownes', a Spanish guitarist played while his wife, a black-haired Irish beauty who wore fire engine-red lipstick, danced flamenco. Avocado, sangria, mango.

We reached Provincetown that afternoon by three. We had drinks, fed each other antipasto and long strands of pasta. We returned to our inn to make love in a strange room in an old town that belonged to my childhood. Our room had cornflower wallpaper, quilted spreads and rag rugs on the floor. Our lovemaking had a contrite quality to it, taking place under the covers, in the dark, quietly so no one would hear us growl.

I woke next morning to Gunnar's voice, low and guarded as he spoke a faulty and complaining French into the telephone, holding the receiver close to his mouth. I felt like the wife of a mafioso. Apparently, his clandestine appointment-making was with Alain, the Silver Fantasy dealer whose store was in town. When he was off the phone I asked if I could accompany him. He seemed surprised that I would want to go, but he agreed. We headed out to Commercial Street where there were more galleries than ever, and just as many souvenir stands. The town suffered from schizophrenia; it could not choose between its grossest desires and its finest instincts.

Alain's storefront had been designed to look like an art gallery, but when you looked closely, only Silver Fantasies hung on the walls. After I'd politely looked around, I sat down to watch Gunnar do business. From what I understood of Gunnar's broken French, Gunnar, a.k.a. the sole representative of Silver Fantasies in the Greater New York Area, argued that he had the right to buy Silver Fantasies selectively, based on how well they sold. But Alain, sole representative of the entire New England States, insisted that Gunnar buy quantity in pre-packed boxes. Alain argued that the boxes offered a standard variety including the best-selling: *high seas under threatening skies, hay fields during harvest, wild geese flying south,* and so on. Gunnar shouted that customers who came to the Provincetown shop were allowed to buy single pictures according to their own taste, why shouldn't he have the same freedom? Ah, explained the Moroccan condescendingly, *this*, Gunnar must understand, was a *gallery*. They shouted back and forth, Gunnar insistent on achieving the upper hand.

Gunnar aggressively pursued his case, thumbing through the boxes, holding up examples of hopelessly unsalable clinkers. He threatened to stop selling Silver Fantasies. *He could sell anything and he would*, he threatened angrily, his blond curls bouncing up and down. To this, Alain frowned, shrugged, waved his hands above his head. As the two of them argued, there was more slipping in and out of French, holding up prints, and pointing at boxes. Finally there was a rustling of papers, columns of numbers were put to paper, additions and subtractions made, pencil points licked, and the whole thing started all over again until both men had rearranged numbers suitably and were satisfied. Then, a final tally on the adding machine and a receipt.

Watching Gunnar pay for his Silver Fantasies was illuminating. I had already noticed that all monies for gas, hotel and restaurants had been paid out of his left leg pocket, what I now realized was his pleasure stash. His right leg pocket, however, was his business bank. A boy who is afraid of losing his pants keeps tightening his belt; a man afraid of losing his money carries it close to his body. Gunnar unfurled hundreds of singles and fanned them in front of Alain's face. Green was his metier. Money was the stuff of his heart.

On the way back to New York, he drove off the road and parked at a scenic rest area, and there we watched the ocean and listened to the cars stream by on their way back home. He played with his cigar, inhaled, then tossed it out the window and took my hand.

"You are quiet," he said.

Why did I have a nagging suspicion that I was about to play "Let's Make a Deal" with Gunnar?

"Look, I am very straightforward guy, very—" He searched for the word. "Very, how you say, X Y Z."

I was already used to his groping English.

"You are, to me, very special. I am very good businessman. You are excellent talent. Together we make love, we make business," he singsonged. "You want to cook for people? You want restaurant? I give you one."

Seduced and propositioned by a lowbrow. From the first kiss in his stale kitchen with the one bare bulb burning into my eyes, I had been wondering where this would lead and what I would do about it.

"My Keetchie," he kissed my fingers one by one, "you think you would like?"

Here was my dream promoter, the man in my corner of the ring. Who cared if I didn't understand him half the time? In twenty years his English would be better than mine, and I would understand every word he said before he said it.

"I have vision of future for us. Together, we can make exceptional life," he added proudly, "We gonna make exciting business. You will see." He stroked my hair and looked into my eyes.

I wondered if this was what love meant to him.

"Please, Keetchie, I don't want to lose you."

Half of Massachusetts must have whizzed past us in their automobiles. My silence was as telling as speech. I had fallen in love with an alien so strange, he might just as well have come from Mars. And now he was proposing. Something or other.

"I don't mean marriage. Anyone can do that. I mean something much more, much greater than marriage."

Okay, bigger than a breadbasket.

"I am talking about making of *life*."

Together and a life, but not a marriage. Could mean maybe a business, maybe a vision, maybe a future. The words hung there like the long ash on a smoldering cigarette.

"You will see. You will see," he promised tenderly. "We make very *good* life together. You will see what we are going to make together."

I was the American, but it was Gunnar who spoke the language. The language of love perfumed ever so sweetly with business.

Five

From the moment we pulled over on that highway of love, we had incorporated. From the very first, our life together was a business. We pooled our monies and shared a booth for the rest of the fair season. Gunnar hung his pictures behind us as a backdrop while I used the tabletop for food. The combination of glittering tableaux and gourmet sandwiches worked well. When we weren't making profits, we made love. On weekdays, Gunnar's hot rod carried us out to Long Island beaches. It was a good life. In the cool fall weather, street fairs came to an end and the old-timers moved on. I thought of following them south, but Gunnar had other ideas. Some of our customers had asked me if I catered.

"Take whatever work you get," Gunnar cheerfully encouraged me. His sales had fallen off, and he was more disenchanted than ever with Silver Fantasies. "Labor Day is gonna be, how you say, big cash windfall. Don't worry, you will get lots help from me."

Gunnar's palate was coated with tar but he could chop like an angel. He seduced garlic out of its skin, peeled potatoes like a marine on KP. The man's mirepoix was a miracle; his dicing, like his lovemaking, yielded abundant results. But as good as he was at wielding a knife, Gunnar had no sense of taste.

"Forget about it, what kind of tongue I'm gonna develop as a kid? Where I grew up was like big snowball factory. What I'm gonna learn on, ice? All over Finland is fabulous cooks, my mother is worst cook, can't butter bread. My whole life food tastes—" He fumbled for words, searching three languages, unable to find the right adjective in his linguistic memory, settling on a simple choice. "My whole life food tastes *like shit*."

He shook his head, "Russian food is *worst* kind food. All time my father and I are in America, we take out Chinese. I am knowing more about Chicken Lo Mein than borscht."

A gustatory illiterate, Gunnar did possess some culinary preferences. He liked to bite into tomatoes rather than slice them, he ate over the sink as though *dish* was a hard concept to warm to. He was a kitchen philosopher, holding forth with his apron on, waving his wooden spoon.

"Icebox, like life, is cold, and always we are bending to it."

I gave him new foods to taste.

"Persimmon—Jesu Christo, such weird stuff. On other hand," he wisely considered, "is very sexy." He ate and thought some more.

"One of these days I gonna cook for you some Russian food and put you to test. One bite week-old cabbage stew, we gonna see what kind stuff you really made of."

He expected me to be the boss in the kitchen. He liked being told what to do, as long as I gave him directions incrementally. He became as exacting as an engineer and as formal as the Czar when he didn't like the way I told him to clarify butter.

"You will, please, show me angle at which ladle is most proficient for removing butter scum."

We prepared food for over fifty people that Labor Day weekend. We arranged three parties successfully, preparing and delivering the food. After our last drop-off, we celebrated in my living room, sitting on the floor, drinking wine and counting our money. First he waved the bills at me, as I'd seen him do with Alain, then he threw them up in the air and covered us with money rain. He was very pleased with both of us.

"I am so happy to make money. I was like bear thinking of long, cold winter. How we gonna get along? This is very good work. We must do more work like this together."

"You want to cook?"

"Don't worry. I can learn. Anything. Languages, cooking. All same thing. Is my best feature." He thumped his chest. "I am Get-Along Cassidy."

I never knew whether his jokes were the product of intelligence or botched acculturation.

"You will see, I will learn to cook. I will be big help for you. It took me long time to find you, you gonna have hard time to get rid of me. I will get so good on stove, I will play like piano. Maybe one day I cook even better than you."

"Piano man, right."

"Don't you see, Keetchie," he explained, "we on our way now. We can do this *together*. We can make move to start restaurant."

The more he pushed, the more skeptical I became. Still, I listened.

"I have plan. We rent house, open up dinner club for guests on weekends. We start small, save money, we get bigger. We are like catering hall in Borough Park. People come to us, we don't go to no one, no more." He made no distinction between cooking and selling corny pictures; work was all the same to him as long as it made money.

"Leesen, we gonna leave this dump, get nice classy house with garden. I got one lined up already. Roumanian guy I know who works for U.N. is moving out of house in Brooklyn Heights. Six rooms, three floors. We can fill with tables and chairs. I am telling you, this is our break. We take it, we start restaurant."

This wasn't exactly what I'd had in mind. "What's the matter with that little luncheonette idea of mine? Warm climate, near water—"

"Hey, we know market here. We are both understanding New York."

"I kind of liked the idea of a cozy little place down south somewhere."

"Why you want to hide? You are big city girl. Take bite of Big Apple."

"A restaurant is a restaurant, a house is a house, Gunnar. There are laws."

"Nobody gonna bother us in Brooklyn. Is no law against weekend dinner club. I check already."

"Forget the cooking, you should be a lawyer."

He paid no attention to me, but steamrolled on, making his point. "And we gonna be cheap too. I got it all figured out. Low overhead. You gonna be famous."

"In Brooklyn?" I didn't believe him, yet I followed along.

"Hey, they go for things like this in Brooklyn." He waved his palms, searching his private dictionary for the right word. "Is big outpost for domestic stuff. Lots of classy peoples is cooking for hobby, want to go out weekends, taste somebody else's cooking. Hey, it's a start. Trust me, we gonna be fine."

Then he told me he had already taken a job to cater a Christmas party. Pot-au-feu for fifty. No problem, he had assured the customer, we had plenty of space in our house in Brooklyn.

"You took a job without even asking me?"

"Hey, you gonna say no, we not gonna do it. Just I wanted to set it up, have it all ready so you can see whole landscape I am painting. Like present. If you like, we do it, if you don't like, we gonna forget whole thing. Never happened, I return guy's money. Hey, he can't sue me, I didn't do nothing wrong yet."

"Pot-au-feu?"

"You made the other night, remember? That soup stuff. It was delicioso. Leesen, in business you got to specialize."

Gunnar wasted no time getting his plan underway. We were out walking over the Brooklyn Bridge by nine the next morning, off to meet our new landlord. It was a beautiful clear autumn day. Gunnar was in high spirits, his chest barreled out, his posture erect, his stride brisk and proud.

"Are you the Grand Marshal or are we walking across this bridge together?"

He would never answer directly to criticism, but he did slow down to my pace. He leaned over the rail and paused to speculate on the wonders of the skyline. He hummed a few stale bars of "I Love New York."

If there were days made for lovers and fools, this was one. The city seemed full of promise, and the polluted river flowed with possibilities. Gunnar looked out towards the water.

"Is all ours, Keetchie."

Gunnar the Hallmark card. Kitsch permeated him like the vein in blue cheese. He cherished the hackneyed; the sight of a Hummel could make him bawl. It followed that he was part peacock. For our walk, he'd worn his cowboy hat. All morning he'd played with the brim, adjusting it jauntily every few minutes till he got it just the way he wanted it, eyes squinting, cigar butt twitching at the corner of his mouth.

"What's with the hat?"

He grinned, blew a smoke ring, then asked vulnerably, "You think is too much for outer boroughs? Makes bad impression on landlord?"

We walked to the outskirts of Brooklyn Heights, passing several Victorian brownstones whose large parlor rooms were filled with period furniture. He stretched out his arms to either side of the tree-lined, cobblestoned streets like Moses in sight of the new land.

"All kinds good money living here. Big jobs, big houses, big kitchens. Middle-class peoples, they love to eat, right?" He stopped short, frowned, drew on his cigar, held it, studied it, and looked at me thoughtfully. "Why is that?"

Chittingham Mews, our new home, was a nineteenth-century mews enclosed by a wrought-iron gate. Each of the twenty-four Chittingham houses had been christened after birds thought to be indigenous to the English countryside. Their names were printed in gold leaf on signs resembling nests over the main entrances. Ours would be The Lark. The houses faced each other in two rows of twelve, like dancers lined up for quadrilles, and shared a formal front garden complete with spouting fountain and large pine tree that doubled as a Christmas tree in the holiday season. Chittingham had a smaller-than-small-town atmosphere in which everyone knew everyone else's business and shared the same interior floor plan.

Our potential landlords were a thirtyish pair, married since they were eighteen years old, currently caught up in a bitter separation fight. Neither would leave the house they both claimed as their own. Divorce horns locked, each lived in three rooms on opposite sides of The Canary. Deedee had kitchen rights, while Ralph had to take all his meals outside the house. I suggested that perhaps one of them ought to take over The Lark rather than rent it to us, but neither Deedee nor Ralph liked this suggestion. Before we left any deposit check, I wanted to make sure that Gunnar's idea of a "weekend dinner club" wasn't news to the already unhappy uncouple. As it turned out, Ralph couldn't boil water and was only too glad to have someone next door who could cook his dinner two or three times a week. Deedee reassured me further.

"I don't give a fuck what you open up next door. Make it a goddamn bordello for all I care. Just pay your rent on time."

In the Heights, ownership was next to godliness, restoration was a religion, and real estate investment was a part of the wedding vows. There was a standing joke about couples who managed to keep their marriage intact through a brownstone renovation, but, like Deedee and Ralph Williams, got divorced once their house was completed. Gunnar and I considered ourselves exempt from this unlucky curse since we were not moving to Brooklyn to worship at the altar of domestic renovation but to start a business.

We filled five of our six rooms with tables and chairs from thrift stores. Gunnar emptied every Salvation Army in five boroughs of dinette sets. He piled mismatched tables and chairs onto his convertible, and, smiling like a hillbilly, he drove the battered furniture back to Brooklyn. We decorated the walls with Gunnar's Americanski collection of Pez holders and political buttons, and hung up my still lifes. We used thick restaurant china from Hot Dog Dukes and Bursting Bob's Beefhouse. Our Home on Chittingham, as we now called it, was funky but serviceable.

Before we opened up for paying customers, I insisted on some run-through dinners, rehearsals with live people.

"Don't worry, I got plenty friends," he said confidently, "and they all hungry."

Gunnar didn't just collect friends, he banked them. Our first patrons were drawn against his expansive friendship account. Gunnar was a model hail-fellow-well-met. He conducted conversation as though it were an orchestra. Our guests included a porno star on the rise named Dolores Del Rio and her boyfriend John, a Golden Gloves boxer whose star was also on the ascendant but whose personal discipline seemed on the wane. Gunnar's friend Frenchie showed up for dinner too.

Frenchie was the personal valet for a transvestite rock and roll group called The Babes. He toured with them and took care of their gowns. When he wasn't on the road with his band, he dressed drag queens, renting them gowns for a fee. He lived in a basement apartment with hundreds of plumbing pipes running along his ceiling, very convenient for hanging up his extensive costume collection. Frenchie had one of those phobic fears of dentists you read about in the *Journal of Modern Psychology* or *Modern Dentistry*. He had no teeth, so for him I had cooked only soft things, poached eggs on mashed potatoes. For dessert we would all eat flan, without the caramel.

Frenchie gave a toothless whistle as he surveyed our living room.

"I get it, Champ, you're a restaurant now!" He looked underneath all the tables and felt the linen on the tablecloths.

"Verrry nice threads, Champ." All of Gunnar's friends called him Champ.

Gunnar also had friends with college degrees, like Rayburn Billy, a medical student from West Virginia. Rayburn, who was studying psychiatry, ate anything that showed up on a plate. And while he ate, he would berate himself for eating too much. The meal was so good, he drawled, he couldn't stop. Rayburn's appetite waged war with his conscience over every bite he took. Too much animal fat, not enough vegetables, too much sugar, not enough carbohydrates. The worse he perceived the food was for him, the more it tempted him.

I had invited my friends Ginger and Wally Willicott, who had been released to his Aunt Dorian's care. The rehearsal dinner seemed a perfect opportunity to see him again. He drank Schweppes through a straw and applauded my efforts at running a restaurant in my home.

"I knew you had it in you. And I like the guy too. Pollack? Great profile. Think he'd model for me one morning? Maybe a patch over one eye, good nose for an aristocratic pirate."

Wally wasn't penitent in the least, though he was sorry he had lost his apartment. Now he lived with Aunt Dorian, who threatened to cut off his trust fund unless he took his Antabuse. He had brought as his date a young Egyptian girl, his aunt's live-in maid Fatima, a beauty with kohl-rimmed eyes. He introduced her as "my little Cleopatra," adding lasciviously, "she squeezes my oranges every morning." Fatima seemed skeptical of Wally's attentions, yet quite proud to be on a date with her American boss. During dinner Wally complained indignantly that though Aunt Dorian had provided him with a bedroom and a sunny studio in her large apartment on West End Avenue, in order to get to it, he had to go through her waiting room, which was always filled with drunks.

Frenchie listened politely to Wally while, with his chin to the table, he slurped the soft specialties of the house: creamed corn soup and curried eggplant custards. Dolores, who had brought me flowers, now ripped into her chicken leg, teeth flaring, lips never touching bird flesh or losing a speck of painted color. When she was done she picked at her cuspids in a manner that guaranteed cinematic fame. Her boyfriend John was a fastidious eater who consumed one thing at a time on the plate, starting with his least favorite, the grilled tomatoes with cilantro butter, because, he explained, it built discipline.

"You cannot *want*," he said. "You cannot want *so much*. It weakens you." John was trying hard to recover his form and get back into his current trainer's good graces.

Dr. Rayburn Billy waxed conversational over the potatoes Dauphinois. "They're so good, I can't eat them. Oh yes, I can. They're filled with everything bad, my arteries are whining. But who cares if I live one week less. If I got hit by a car tomorrow, this meal could be the nearest I'd ever get to heaven."

Ginger, round cheeks flushed with wine, proved once again that she could get chummy with a telephone pole. She discussed the differences between Clorox and generic bleach with Dolores who was interested in removing chocolate stains from white cotton blouses. She conducted a long interview with Frenchie on silk versus taffeta and asked him if the petticoat worn by Scarlett's maid in *Gone with the Wind* was located in the Smithsonian. After she explained what the Smithsonian was, she chugged along full throttle, engaging Dr. Billy in a debate concerning the long-range effectiveness of thorazine, to dope or not to dope.

"Where do you get this stuff," I whispered as I cleared her entree. "What do you know about schizophrenics?"

"Oh, *please*," she waved my compliment away modestly, "supermarket psychology. Sooner or later, *McCall's* tells you everything."

The evening was a big success. "Gunnar's a people wizard," Rayburn assured me as he left. "He's going to be a goddamn Merlin with John Q. Public." Dolores offered Gunnar a tongue kiss.

"You were such a hot waiter, I should tip you." Her hands traveled down the sides of his body, stuffing a bill in his hip pocket. Gunnar pulled away laughing and declined the gratuity. For such an opportunist, Gunnar was surprisingly faithful.

Now that our rehearsal dinner had gone smoothly, it was time to consider the logistics of opening up. Gunnar envisioned the big picture. He wasted no time, and the next morning over a cup of coffee, he handed me a flyer to read and explained proudly, "Xerox, ten cents."

Chittingham Mews Private Dining Club

Pot-Au-Feu our specialty

Bring your own wine and beer

$10.50 for four-course dinner

Kitterina Kittridge, Chef

Our Home on Chittingham is private dining club for gourmet type eaters. Our chef is coming from fine old tradition of European cooks. Enjoy fine dining in casual home atmosphere. Plenty tables and chairs. And friends, don't forget to bring booze to cut cost of dinner!

As far as Gunnar was concerned, all I had to do was correct his English and fill in menu, time, place and price. I had a few questions, however.

"I don't know if I'm ready for this."

"You ready, already. Don't you *want* to sell you cooking?"

"But what if this plan of yours doesn't work?"

"Jesu Christo, you not knowing good PR when you seeing it!"

"What's this 'fine tradition of European cooks' stuff, anyway?"

"Sounds good, no?"

"Gunnar, it can't just *sound* good, it has to be *real*. You're supposed to tell the public the truth. I'm an American, I don't have a traditional bone in my body."

"Leesen, you grew up around art and museums, and now I am in your life. Don't worry, you got plenty foreign influence."

We ate our Sunday breakfast in silence.

"So, you gonna try, right?"

He started rubbing my neck and kissing my ears.

"I'm gonna make you very happy," he crooned.

We went back upstairs to bed and made love.

Gunnar's public relations campaign had started during the summer when, with a smile as inviting as an ear of corn, he had encouraged customers to add their names to our mailing list.

"What mailing list?" I had objected. "I don't even own an address book."

"Trust me, one day we gonna *need* mailing list and we gonna *have* it." That summer he collected a list of over one thousand people and now each one of them would receive a flyer about Out Home on Chittingham.

Gunnar never left the house without stuffing flyers in his pockets to give away on his way to the dry cleaner, the library, the subway. He campaigned the streets so fervently that one old woman promised to vote for him. Our reservations for the following weekend began to add up; we had twenty reservations for Saturday, fifteen for Sunday. Gunnar's vision took shape.

When it came to drumming up business, Gunnar was a Tartar. He called diners who had eaten with us and wrested from them the names of not just one or two friends who might be interested in having dinner in our home, but five or six. He was greedy for success and hit the campaign trail again and again, papering the streets with our newest menus. He made friends with antique dealers, oriental carpet dealers, automotive and transmission specialists, or teachers at local elementary schools. Gunnar made everyone feel right at home. He removed a coat like an old friend and sat a guest down like a brother. When he poured people their own liquor, he made them feel they were drinking out of his own private coffers. By that winter we were feeding as many as thirty people a night, but as our business grew, so did our troubles with Chittingham Mews.

Six

The Chittingham Mews was split over the Our Home issue. Some neighbors ate with us on weekends, while others gossiped and mounted a campaign against us. By January the conflict between neighbors who came to dinner and those who would not took a serious turn.

Garbage was the issue. Benny Costanza was the villain.

It began one day as we were taking out a bag of garbage. Benny, who was hanging out his laundry to dry on the clothesline, looked at us and shook his head.

"If you was a real restaurant, you'd be onna street inna store, like with everybody else who's got a real restaurant. *Onna street, inna store.*" He kept repeating this mantra, shaking his head that such an abomination as Our Home had happened in his own backyard.

Temperatures dropped, snow fell, an envelope was shoved under our kitchen door. An envelope of doom, it had ultimatum written all over it.

To Whom It May Ever Concern,
This is to serve notice on the inhabitants of Twelve Chittingham
Mews, a.k.a. The Lark of which said building in resides one

*Gunnar Gunnarson and another Kitterina Kittridge. Please
be so advised that a goodly number of neighbors here are sick of
your illegal practices and plan to notify all such agencies, like the
sanitation and garbage departments, to render you illegal to
continue your business at aforesaid address. Be so advised, we
don't like it and we're going to get you in the end. Cease and de-
sist from running your dining club in our backyard and all
your other illegal practices. You have three weeks before all such
agencies like the police and board of health are notified.*

> *Signed, Your neighbors who won't eat
> at your place and who you have not seen
> fit to take into any consideration.*

*P.S. You don't have a liquor license and we know you don't pay
taxes either. So who's kidding who?*

> *Signed, Concerned Neighbors for a
> Clean Chittingham Mews*

"It's not like we can hire a lawyer, Gunnar, we have no case.
They'd laugh us right out of court."

"Chrissakes, this guy's English is worse than mine, even."
Gunnar rubbed his fingers over his chin. "Okay, okay, so we are
screwed. But we had good run, don't get upset. We had long
time here. Was good test drive for next place we gonna open. I
start to look tomorrow. We gonna find right place, don't
worry." He rubbed my arm and kissed my shoulders. Business
decisions were foreplay to our lovemaking. "Customers gonna
follow us, you will see."

Then, in a typically Gunnarian way, he added, "Best thing
ever happened to us, getting kicked out of Mews. Could be
start of something big, finally."

We showed the letter to our next-door neighbor Frank Dearborne.

"Well, my loves, you are rather *outre*, but so many of us like that about you. This was a dull place before you two arrived on the scene." Frank adjusted his red bifocals, lips moving as he read the letter.

"Hmm, clouded mafioso threats from that little pepperoni. Well, I suppose I should give Benito some credit for having even this much courage in him. All this trouble from a post office retiree, his wife and her sister. Well, well, well, Benny, Rose and Pearl, vipers of the alley, I never knew they had it in them." Frank handed us back the letter and thoughtfully played with the leonine charm that hung from his neck.

"I'll spy a little and see if I can find out what they're up to."

Frank called a few days later. "No pun intended," he snorted, "but they're cooking up something. It'll happen in the next few weeks, but I'm damned if I can figure out what it is. The other side won't talk. Be careful, you two. I smell a rat."

It snowed every day that week. On Friday afternoon, new snow fell on top of old snow, schools were closed, and, as luck would have it, garbage pickups were canceled because of striking sanitation men. Outside the gates of Chittingham Mews, large, industrial-strength black plastic bags piled upon one another. They hadn't looked very pretty during the first few days of the strike, and four more inches of snow hadn't improved them.

That weekend we planned to serve scallops in lime and ginger butter, blanquette de veau, salad, cheese, and for dessert, a caramel apple tartin. Not the most imaginative menu, but good for a cold night in the middle of winter. Snowstorm notwithstanding, the house was booked. It was going to be a busy weekend. I trudged through the snow, doing my shopping. The scene at the fish store was one I had lived before.

"Ernie, I ordered bay scallops, *bay*, remember?"

"Listen, I'm not the king of the sea. I take what I can get."

"The customers are paying for bay scallops, Ernie," I warned.

"Listen, they're not the king of the sea either. Do you want these sea scallops or should I put them on as a special and hope I move 'em?"

Enough said. I took my scallops and went on to Stukie's the butcher, where I anguished over buying ten pounds of veal versus twelve, opted for the twelve just in case we got some last-minute reservations, worried about what twenty dollars extra would do to my profit margin if no extra customers called up.

Stukie was a big man in his forties, handsome if you overlooked his left ear that had been ripped off by a dog or a horse or another marine. Stukie was a human junkyard dog. He made his real money in local real estate, and he was always on the phone with a plumber while he hacked away at your meat order. He was fond of reminding his customers that he only stayed in the meat business because he liked it. He had a coarse, booming voice and a laugh that sounded like sobbing. He insisted his son, a scrawny ten year old, work with him every day after school. The kid hated everything in his father's store, including the sawdust. The tension between them made visits to Stukie's like a brief sentence in a meat penitentiary, and I was always glad to escape.

At four in the afternoon, I received a call from a party of four who claimed they had sent in their check and reconfirmed their dinner reservations. The same thing happened with another two and then another four. I wondered if our Chittingham enemies had tampered with our mail. At the Mews, mailboxes were never locked.

It was too late to get more meat from Stukie's. Besides, even if I had the meat, where would I get the three hours to stew it? The twelve pounds would just have to travel a little further than I'd expected.

I was thinking about the miracle of loaves and fishes when my mother called. Lilly had decided to come tonight to see Our Home and to meet Gunnar, both for the first time. Why couldn't she have invited us over for brunch if she wanted to check up on my lover? Gunnar wanted to meet her.

"Why you are so worried? She will love me. I make you mother very proud to have such nice live-in-law."

The phone rang again at six. It was our neighbor Paula who usually helped Gunnar wait on tables. She was in bed with the flu and wouldn't be able to come to work that evening. Customers were due to arrive at seven. We spent the next half hour on the phone trying, without success, to find a friend who could help out. So far, evenings at Our Home had all been successful, so maybe we were immune to disasters. And maybe the moon was a Roquefort soufflé.

I climbed the stairs to our bedroom on the third floor where Gunnar was taking apart our bed, putting away the headboard, and rolling up our foam-rubber mattress into the closet to make room for more tables and chairs. On my way up to get dressed for the evening, I looked at our rooms. The sun had set, the harsh afternoon light had gone, replaced now by the long shadows of evening. The flickering light of gas lamps in the front courtyard shined through the curtained windows onto the tables, adding more romance and mystery to the dining process than it probably deserved.

I changed into clean clothes and a new apron, and on my way back down to the kitchen, I heard a commotion outside in front of our house. People's voices chanted loudly above the scrunch of snow shovels clearing the walk. I looked out the window and saw a small crowd of neighbors holding placards, protesting Our Home on Chittingham. They were dressed in their warmest clothes, having come prepared for a long vigil in the enemy camp. They were stamping their feet and waving their placards. The slogans were meant to inspire indigestion and discourage customers from walking into Our Home.

It's ten o'clock, do you know where your salmonella is?

Mews for residents, not rodents!

Call the Board of Health! Sign our petition! Return Chittingham Mews to sanity!

The protestors had dragged several of our garbage bags in front of the stairs to our house where, like shiny black gargoyles, they blocked customers from coming upstairs into Our Home.

I leaned my head against the cold windowpane and looked past the protesters to the brightly lit Christmas tree in the center of the courtyard. This was going to be the most humiliating evening of my life. Gunnar bounded outside, removed the garbage bags, bullied the protesters into stepping aside. I took people's coats as soon as they walked inside. The noisy demonstration made our bastard cafe seem more of a Quasimodo creature than ever.

"What kind of place is this, anyway?" one woman asked, clutching her two bottles of Chardonnay as she entered the house.

The requests began for glasses of water, decanters, highball glasses, tissues. Before I knew it, people were complaining that there was no more toilet paper in the bathroom. Everyone wanted wine, so Gunnar started handing out corkscrews. "Here," he smiled at a dumbfounded guest. "And when you done opening yours, you gonna help other guy open his."

I hadn't even gotten around to serving the first course yet. I ran to the kitchen and started feeding scallops to the broiler god. Like any offering, I hoped it would bring about order. Instead, my mother, in mink caftan, beaver snow bonnet and rubber overshoes, walked in through the back door of the kitchen, Perrier bottle in hand. At least it was a twist-off.

Gunnar dispensed a hearty welcome and handshakes. He was glad of the commotion; it meant success.

"So," Lilly took Gunnar's hand coolly, "you are celebrities in your own backyard."

"Sure. And we gonna move to bigger space soon too," Gunnar said proudly as he took her coat and led her to a small table on the second floor.

Even Gunnar was no match for this evening. We ran up and down the stairs as people asked for extra napkins, clean forks, sharp knives, more bread, more water. One woman said her feet were cold, could she borrow a hot water bottle and did we have an extra pair of woolen socks? We ran out of ice cubes just as the appetizers were served; the hard liquor fans threatened to join the protestors.

I practically threw the entrees onto plates. I had enough blanquette de veau for thirty but somehow when I reached plate number twenty-six, there was no meat left.

"Wait, I gonna fix this." Gunnar left the kitchen and returned with four plates full of stew. He scraped some off the top of each plate. "This table never gonna miss it. I told them their plates looked cold, I'm gonna take back to kitchen to heat up."

When I objected, he said, "Forget it, they so drunk out of minds, they can't tell veal from breadsticks." I heated the rest of the stew in the skillet and plopped it onto eight plates which Gunnar sped out of the kitchen, presto. When he returned to the kitchen I asked, "So, how's it going with my mother?"

His eyes widened, and I knew he'd forgotten her at her table in the hard-to-get-at corner on the second floor. By this time, all the blanquette de veau was gone, with just a few baby onions and turnips sitting in some already extended cream sauce. I showed Gunnar the bottom of the pot and started to cry.

"Leesen, Keetchie, put some of that chopped green stuff—"

"Parsley?"

"On top, yeah, like that, and put on tofu stuff you made for our dinner last night. She's gonna love it. We charge her double for vegetarian special."

I wanted this evening to be over. My legs ached, my back hurt, I'd sprained a wrist wiping so many glasses. I wanted to sleep in my bed, but I'd have to wait till people stopped eating in my bedroom before I could crawl into the closet to retrieve my mattress.

I helped clear the entree dishes while people clamored for the next course. We ran up and down the stairs, like human centipedes, balancing plates. The sink was piled so high with dishes there was no room for more, so I opened up the back door to the alley and started piling them outside in the backyard. The snow swallowed them up and turned them into snow midgets. All I needed was for Benny Costanza to come along. But he was so busy waving placards in the front garden, chances were good he wouldn't show up back here. At least not for a while. And if he did, so what? This evening couldn't possibly get any worse.

We were up to the salad and cheese course. Naturally there wasn't enough lettuce, so I opened up my vegetable bin and grabbed anything green. Let them eat spinach, I muttered as I poured on the dressing, filled the plates with fistfuls of greens.

The snowdrifts were getting larger. Around dessert time, the picketers had finally gone home, like a tired mariachi band, having serenaded us long enough. Some customers didn't notice anything was wrong. It was that time in the evening when guests grew chummy with the persons sitting in the same room with them. Brandies were sampled and shared as I looked for clean glasses and snifters. Fat chance. The pile of dishes in the garden had grown into an architectural feat rivaling Pisa.

I ducked into the bathroom, fixed my hair, and then went to my mother's table. I wanted to know if she had liked dinner. *No, I didn't.* I wanted to know if she had liked Gunnar. *No, I didn't.* I wanted to know if she liked what I had done with my life, as though she were a reliable yardstick.

She was finishing her coffee. I sat down.

"So," my mother shrugged, "is he stupid or is it just poor command of English?"

After lifelong encounters with the public, how had Lilly remained so artless in her dealings with people? Having said her piece, Lilly tried to behave, conceding that some horrible things were better than other horrible things and this catastrophe had its bright side.

"You *could* be taking drugs and living in hallways."

Gunnar joined us, and we listened as my mother described a

charcoal study for a minor Sloane she was considering purchasing. She grilled Gunnar, found out he had studied engineering, and extracted a promise from him to "come round" and fix a broken hallway light in her foyer. She left before the other guests, managing to summon a taxi even on a night like this. Lilly stood in the snowy garden waving goodnight, looking as morose as a character in a Chekhov play. "I don't understand it, but I suppose that doesn't matter anymore."

"Lilly, I know how hard this is for you—" I said.

"No, you don't. You don't have a clue." She trundled off to her taxi.

Around 2:00 A.M., people started to leave, and the smell of wet boots, wet woolen scarves and thank yous once again filled the air.

"Even the protesters were great."

"Yeah, neat touch."

I smiled weakly. The moon shone brightly over the garbage bags. We brought the dishes back from the yard in icy clumps. Spoons were frozen to plates. The snowy path around our kitchen door was brown with gravy. We turned out the lights, too tired to talk. We trudged up the stairs to bed.

We both heard it at the same time. A slow, relaxed wheeze that grew louder as we approached the upstairs bedroom. We carried the tables out of our bedroom, still trying to place the sound. We were too tired to put up the bed again and decided to sleep on the floor. I opened up the closet door to recover our mattress, and a man fell out.

It was little Charlie Deitz, the third-grade teacher from table number five, second floor, the one who'd asked for seconds on every course. He was a small, sandy-haired man who rubbed his eyes and adjusted his wire glasses which were bent out of shape from sleeping on them and made his tired face look a cross between Silly Putty and Mr. Potato Head. He'd fallen asleep at the table and hadn't wanted to disturb the rest of his party, so he'd crawled up here just like Goldilocks and found what he needed, a foam-rubber roll, tucked neatly away in this closet. Talk about comfortable, it was just like the one he slept on in his own home. By the way, had we seen his wife? She had left without him? No matter. Would we mind getting him a drink of water, and would it be all right if he spent the night? He took his coffee black and had to be up for work by seven.

"Come on, buddy," said Gunnar, "I take you home. Special service, no charge."

"Really, don't go to any bother," said Charlie, in no rush to get home to a wife who had forgotten to collect him. "Couldn't I just bed down for the night in your living room?"

I shook my head. We did not own a couch.

Seven

Gunnar hit the streets to find a restaurant for rent. He left home every morning like a three-star general ready for action, the *New York Times* stuck under his arm like a paper rifle, a list of appointments as long as his face.

"I feel fire inside me to move, can't lose momentum. Is imperative to start new business right away." The longer his search continued, the more Gunnar sounded like an urgent telegram.

He came home each night to report on the places he had seen: abandoned butcher shops, hot dog stands closed down by the Board of Health, bodegas with good plumbing but no floors. Every few days we would look together at the best of what he had found: old Cantonese kitchens and delis whose white-haired owners eyed us hopefully as we toured their shops. Nothing could have been more cautionary than inspecting old, failed restaurants. Still, like intrepid romantics, we wandered hopefully through countless kitchens. All the spaces were wrong, none of the deals were right. Too much money up front, too much money per month, too big an electric bill, too many improvements needed. Finally, Gunnar came home unexpectedly early one afternoon.

"Get your coat and come with me." He smiled.

"Is this our appointment with destiny, or are you just buying me lunch?"

"Hurry up," he coaxed while handing me my sweater. "Right over bridge is fantastic place, great opportunity."

"The last time you said this, we ended up getting served eviction papers," I mumbled as I stepped into a taxi that brought us over the bridge into lower Manhattan by the East River, into a desolate strip of warehouses and factories, just another up-and-coming Soho border town.

The smell of the river wafted in the breeze.

Henkelbottle's was a two-story, redbrick building with fifteen-foot windows on either side of its corner storefront. Its century-old turrets were copper, and gargoyles looked down from the roof at the hand-carved mahogany doors.

I pointed to the heavy links hanging from the door handles.

"Is anyone showing up to open this place for us, or are we just waiting around for someone to come and shoot us?"

I had to admit, he had found a beautiful place.

"Owner is coming soon. I wanted to be early, just you and me," he purred.

I heard romance. But was the warmth in his voice for me or Henkelbottle's? He hoisted me up onto his shoulders, and I peered through the big window, most of which was covered by a large, yellow, greasy curtain hanging askew from a bent rod. The parted drapes revealed a large, dark, theatrical space, a long, curved bar at the end of the room that bowed out like a stage. Chairs sat on top of some tables, others were overturned on the floor. The place looked like a murky backdrop for an old foreign movie without subtitles.

George Zinker was a willowy man whose spikes of thin hair

stood up on his head as though he'd stuck his finger into an electric outlet and forgotten to take it out. The rest of him was as rumpled as an unmade bed. As he came forward shakily to accept my hand, he seemed shell-shocked, a soldier of capitalism scarred by the battles of business. He was obsessed with the details of his nightmarish failure and couldn't stop talking about them. He seemed to need solace even more than he needed a deal. A computer programmer by day, George had tried to run his bar as a community center where groups on either side of the gentrification fence could mix. Instead, under his management, the bar had become a mecca for junkies and drug dealers.

"Call me crazy—in those days I had a social conscience."

But these days all George had were bills. The heavy chains clanked as he unlocked the doors.

"Security." He shrugged. "Nothing a big dog wouldn't fix."

We walked into a time warp, twilight zone material, as Henkelbottle's ghost beckoned us. The room smelled of stale hops and rancid soda syrup. It looked hastily deserted. Tables lay on their sides, chairs were flung about the floor. Above, angels and doves reigned at the center of the twenty-foot-high ceiling and looked down at the dissipation below. The walls were covered with dark wooden panels to match the bar on which small demons with forked tails were carved into a palm leaf motif. A floor-to-ceiling beveled mirror provided a dramatic backdrop to the bar and doubled the sunlight that poured into the room through the picture windows. Above the entrance, stained glass panels cast colorful jeweled patterns along the old, splintery floor. The place was a gem, but George had to unload it. He ran his hand over the smooth bar so wistfully, it might have been the body of a woman.

The electricity had been turned off, so George showed us around the dark, musty kitchen with a flashlight. It was a long, narrow, under-equipped space. It consisted of an old Vulcan stove whose broken hinges made the doors of both oven compartments fall like lead weights when opened, a shaky wooden table covered with red vinyl linoleum, a twenty-year-old Sears freezer with missing shelves and mildewed innards, a walk-in refrigerator reeking of old socks and rotten eggs, and a pot rack holding a few dented aluminum pans, the bottoms of which were black with soot. I pulled the shade up. The kitchen faced a brick wall. The walls were the color of LePage's glue. This was definitely not the small country cafe I'd had in mind a few months ago when I catered the streets and dreamed of Miami.

The upstairs apartment, one large, loft-like room, was not much better, though the light was good, and if you stuck your head out the window and craned your neck, you could almost see the river. George assured us that the waterfront was changing. Real estate would soar, and this was the time to get in on a good thing. He would introduce us to the right people who were clamoring for a good restaurant. "The vibes are right," George promised. "You just can't get property like this for the price. Not to mention the apartment right above the store, very convenient."

The deal was colored by George's desperation to unload something he didn't want and by Gunnar's desperation to have it. George wanted money down so he could pay his most pressing debts. He would allow a low rent the first year that would escalate during the second and third years at a high rate to encourage us, by financial arm-twisting, to buy the building.

"If you're not a success by then, you'll never be," George assured us with expertise.

It was the second time I'd seen Gunnar talk money. This time it was not cold cash he was offering but promissory notes. When finally we all agreed to agree, we closed the deal on the spot.

"Congratulations, you're in the restaurant business," smiled George as he shook our hands and took our partial deposit. "It's your problem now."

All we had to do was come up with the rest of the down payment.

We turned to friends for help.

"You did *what*? Champ, you use a lawyer for a deal like that. Why didn't you stop him, Kitchie?" Rayburn Billy lectured us.

Rayburn insisted on seeing Henkelbottle's. He surveyed the room, hands on hips, shaking his head. Obviously the bar hadn't cast the same spell over him as it had us.

"It's a pigsty. How are you two ever going to get this place cleaned up and open for business?"

"You gonna help us," explained Gunnar. "We gonna give you big brush, and we gonna have cleaning party. You are coming, yes?"

"In between classes and rounds at the hospital, right, I'll just scrub up and lend a hand."

"Hey, if you gonna so feel guilty not to help us, write a check instead. We not fussy. We take VISA. "

Ask people you know and love to invest in you and suddenly friends become studies in hardship, family members become judges. Nothing is more humiliating than begging relatives and close friends for money, except, of course, telling them what you want to use their money for. The only thing more mortifying is being turned down. We asked everyone we knew, even Gunnar's Aunt Magrid.

Aunt Magrid lived in a dark apartment, a third-floor walk-up in Brighton Beach. When we arrived she had the table set with an embroidered tablecloth, tea and sticky buns. We three sat down with such solemn formality, we might have been diplomats negotiating a treaty. Magrid sipped her tea and listened carefully to her nephew. There was some polite, curious, though not very animated discussion in Russian. I sat quietly, searching Aunt Magrid's eyes for signs of willingness to part with her rubles. More tea, more Russian. Then somber silence. She had a Dutch-girl clock in her kitchen, the kind where the little Dutch girl wears a pointy hat and her aproned stomach tells the time and her pendulum legs go back and forth like she's dancing, meanwhile the clock is ticking. Time was the only thing I understood about this visit.

Aunt Magrid held her chin, looked me up and down, shook her head sadly, and then suddenly clapped her hands against her old thighs and said, "Da," decisively. She got up, walked to a jar she kept on a shelf above the refrigerator, opened it, and pulled out a hunk of cash as thick as a grapefruit. She counted one thousand dollars which she handed over to Gunnar. Then she patted him on the back as though condolences were in order, crossed herself vehemently, and promptly showed us the door.

I had a hard time keeping up with Gunnar as he raced to the subway. Was he running to our next appointment or away from the one we'd just had?

"Why do I feel we've just visited the kingpin of the Russian mafia rather than your old aunt? What did you tell her the money was for?" I panted.

"I will tell you another time. Right now, we go put this in bank account."

"She just gave it to you, just like that?"

"She is loaning it to me."

"Well, what did you tell her it was for?"

"Not now. You will not like, and I don't want to tell you."

"That bad?"

"Is just loan, is nothing, Chrissakes."

"Why didn't you tell her the truth?"

"My father already asked. Restaurant is bad risk, my aunt said."

"So you told her—"

"Is for abortion."

He quickened his pace. I caught up to him. We were at the subway entrance.

"Should it bother me that a family member would help us get *rid* of something we made rather than *invest* in something we *wanted* to make?"

Gunnar bit his lip nervously. He didn't like it when I talked about things he found too painful to think about.

"Don't dwell, Kitchie. This is *the business of business*. You do whatever you must to begin."

Aunt Magrid remained the one relative who loaned us money. I did not ask my mother, who did not offer either. Lilly had stopped fighting me about what I wanted, but she wouldn't help me. She had adopted a wait-and-see attitude. Wait for me to come to my senses and see that she was right. Halfheartedly, she had accepted Gunnar as a kind of handyman since, as he had promised, he had dutifully shown up at her apartment and fixed her hallway light. Since then, their conversations had moved past light bulbs into hardware, air conditioners and toasters.

Gunnar's father, on the other hand, donated a small van he had fixed in his garage. A tall, dour, silent man with stooped shoulders and thinning gray hair, he hardly ever spoke to me. He spoke to his son in Russian. It sounded less like language, more just the universal grunts of fathers and sons.

"I didn't expect him to give money. I don't think he has any. Horses, cards, dice." Gunnar shrugged by way of explanation, wiggling his fingers to indicate a bogey monster. "Is in our blood."

In addition to Magrid's thousand, Ginger gave us one thousand, and Dr. Billy gave us two more. We were still short of our down payment, but George let us start fixing up the bar anyway.

We bought a drum of Murphy's Oil soap. We polished the wood paneling, swept, mopped, waxed, and shined every surface in the barroom. We couldn't afford epoxy paint to cover the gummy kitchen walls, and as hard as I scrubbed, I couldn't remove stains of unknown origin: flying ketchup, gravy, old coffee grinds. I had once pictured myself cooking in a light and airy room, breeze wafting in through a window, the curtains billowing, my pies cooling in the whitewashed heart of my small-town restaurant. Now I was glad for a few dented pans.

Friends offered us what they could. John-the-Boxer offered to be our bouncer on weekends, Frenchie offered to check coats, Ginger, who was starting social-work school in the fall, said she'd answer phones and take reservations on Saturdays. Wally asked his Aunt Dorian for money for us, but she turned us down.

"With kind, firm WASP warmth, her stock in trade," Wally reported. Instead of giving money, Wally painted the dining room walls for us.

"Found the perfect color today," he announced. "Dollar-bill green mixed with olives." He also touched up the angels on the ceiling, painting in their eyes and applying gold leaf to their wings. Fatima, scared of heights, crouched beside her man on the scaffold, holding his jars of paint and handing him his brushes.

"Number three, sable, please, then number four, flat bristle."

With her devoted concentration to Wally and his brushes, and dressed in her white caftan and gold balgha slippers, Fatima looked like a cross between an Egyptian princess and a dental assistant.

"This is probably the closest I'll ever get to heaven," Wally sighed loudly while painting on his back. "But it adds significantly to my understanding of Tiepolo."

We had many cleaning parties. Henkelbottle's drank gallons of Spic-n-Span and ate five mops.

"I've been thinking," said Frenchie, as he took down the heavy, mustard-colored drapes and measured the windows for the lace curtains he would sew for us. "Seeing as how this place looks so different now than when you first got it, if this restaurant thing don't work out, you guys should consider changing your line of work. Cleaning is a major service, very honorable, nothing to be ashamed of. There's a lot of money in cleaning houses. I know, my mother was in that line of work."

"Yeah," offered Dolores, who had just walked in. "I hear ammonia futures shot up since you two moved in here. I mean, are you two serious? This place is a sewer."

Gunnar handed her a yellow rubber glove.

"Baby, you know I don't do rubber unless it's in front of a camera." Dolores waved a piece of paper, disgruntled. "I just came to drop off my check." She slapped it against his groin and kept her hand there. Inches away from his face, she never took her eyes off his.

"If you bomb, Champ, *you* get to pay off the tab. Maybe you can cook and clean for me for a few months like the happy little caretaker you are," Dolores added.

"Personally, I'd rather eat linoleum," said Rayburn Billy, blowing Dolores a kiss goodbye from across the room where he was shining mirrors.

It was Dolores Del Rio's ten thousand dollars that made the difference between never opening and opening. We handed over our down payment to George and signed the lease. We opened the restaurant a month later.

The neon light flashed on and off. *Kittridge's*, in hot pink and bold green. You could see it from blocks away.

"You're sure you don't want your name up there too?" I had asked.

"Kitchie, you are artist here. I am just—" he hesitated, "I am just *enabler*."

"That's what they call an addict's partner."

"Ahh," he said, thinking this over as he switched the neon sign on and off to make sure it worked. "Yes, well, this is possible."

People strolling in the warm summer twilight looked into our window, read our menu, came in for a drink or an espresso. The place generated a lot of goodwill, and at the end of our first evening of business, we were high on neighborly good wishes. Then Gunnar sat down at a back table and counted the scanty receipts.

"So, Kitchie, now we gonna see what all these handshakes is adding up to." He winked and raised his glass of beer.

"Ching ching," he toasted me, with the imitation ring of a cash register. He counted, then spread the money out on the table like a deck of cards.

"Eighty-nine dollars and eighty-four cents." He took a long sip, finished his beer, and brought the bottle down on the table with a bang.

"Jesu Christo, we gonna be buried alive in shits if this keeps up."

He regained self-possession.

"Okay, we are open. A-plus for us, big pat on back. But now is second tier challenge, to *stay open*."

The coach had rallied the team. I returned to the kitchen to finish washing dishes. Gunnar put out the garbage.

For the next two weeks we served only ten to fifteen dinners on weeknights, here and there an occasional lunch. Passersby and customers from our mailing list brought us thirty to forty people on Fridays and Saturdays. The combined receipts were not enough to carry us. We had only enough savings for two months' rent, so Gunnar took a job driving an all-night delivery truck to make sure we could pay our bills. Gunnar would leave for work at three in the morning, return after lunch, sleep until five, when he would appear in Kittridge's wearing clean chinos and a white oxford shirt. Instant waiter.

"Very American, no?" He modeled the new uniform he had chosen for himself. "Brooks Brothers," he explained seriously as he looked at himself in the floor-to-ceiling mirror behind the bar. "I think is very reassuring look for customers."

Gunnar's answer to keeping any drug traffic away was to sweep in front of Kittridge's any chance he got. "Is war. Must make drug bastards feel unwelcome. We sweep to hold our place. This is not their corner anymore. We sweep." But when Gunnar went to work, there was no one to sweep. I was too busy in the kitchen. Without broom action, the number of addicts and drunks requesting toilet privileges in the bar increased. George Zinker had said a big dog could fix anything, so I went out and got one.

It was Friday, late afternoon. By the time I reached the local Humane Society, I had only fifteen minutes to choose man's best friend before closing time. No time for mistakes. Forget researching breeds, taking a few weeks to ponder the merits of huskies over terriers or retrievers. This was war.

"Pick a cute one, and if he doesn't work out, return him," suggested the director, who read the cage tags dispassionately as we walked through canine death row.

"Let's see, here's one, barks loud, doesn't like children. This here dog likes cats. Does blind in one eye bother you? Wait a second, this here's a good buy. Here, meet Ralph." Retriever tail, collie snout with a long black scar.

"Looks mean enough for what you want," he said. "Especially 'round the nose. Neutered too," he continued, like a car salesman describing the extras on a Chevy. "Loyal. You're all he's got."

"He doesn't bark?"

"You don't hear him, do you?

"He's friendly?"

"He's licking your hand like candy, ain't he?"

He had Gunnar's blond coloring.

"Does he like riding in cars?"

He looked again at the information card. "Loves cars, prefers the back seat. Hates crossing streets."

"I'll take him." I signed the necessary papers as Ralph pulled on the leash. He was eager to put the past behind him and get to work.

The dog understood his job description perfectly. He slept behind the bar, and when necessary, he stood up on his hinds like a canine bartender. It was against health codes to keep a dog in a restaurant, but bathroom traffic decreased considerably. The dog became a local celebrity as more and more customers chose to sit at Ralph's bar to eat their lunch or drink their beer. Beautiful yet scarred, a dog with an obvious past, Ralph fit right in at Kittridge's.

Business increased. Whether due to our four-legged talisman, our food, or our atmosphere, neighborhood regulars came all week long to brood alone or celebrate together. Our weekend reservations were peppered with doctors and dentists. The mix of people worked, especially at the cash register. I had never seen Gunnar so happy. We paid our bills, and by August, Gunnar had quit his trucking job, devoting all his time to Kittridge's.

A restaurant is a noisy, social, moving creature. Bodies huddled around a table, heads bent into plates, outstretched legs taking up twice the space allotted them, arms waving for waiters. Our numbers grew steadily that summer, and by fall we had hired a wait staff who knew the difference between red and white wine.

I kept the menu small at first. Five entrees, four appetizers, three desserts. During May and June, I functioned on inspiration. I cooked what made me happy: plump little trouts sizzling around in a pan, jumping to my tune, getting with the program. Food spoke to my fingers. Shelves of spices, bags of carrots and celery, pounds of beef and other assorted raw flesh called out to me. The sweet aroma of roasted peppers filled the air like marijuana. I breathed deeply the smell of success.

Nothing matched my endless thinking about food, except my endless thinking about love.

Eight

By August, my one-woman kitchen groaned under Kittridge's mounting numbers. I told myself that organization was everything. Each day I wrote a list of what I had to prepare. I used red pens and green pens and underlined things in blue and made out strict and scary schedules with which I browbeat myself. Then I'd start the cooking. Time versus priorities. What to do first? Boil water to blanch the brussels sprouts? Split the chicken breasts? Filet the flounder? Brown the beef and start the stock? The art of cooking became the art of beating the clock. Behind every dish there lurked ten jobs. I no longer had the time to read cookbooks or wander through markets. I was taffy pulled between cooking, answering phones, taking reservations, washing dishes and serving occasional lunch customers whose orders I took and whose food I cooked.

Everything seemed to move too quickly for me; plates of food were cooked and eaten, chairs emptied, then filled again with new customers. Smoke from the grill filled my chest like the inhalation of a hundred Lucky Strikes. I forgot to order flour and eggs one day; the next, crates of butter melted and milk soured outside the walk-in refrigerator. Celery died, lettuce wilted, carrots went rubbery, wheels of cheese spoiled, soup went rancid. My virus spread to the stove as veal sausages slid out of sauté pans, missing the plate by several inches and slithering pathetically onto the floor, and veal cutlets jumped suicidally off their plates as soon as I put them on the pass-through for waiters to pick up. Pans wouldn't heat, water wouldn't boil. Food wouldn't cook for me anymore. My life was a kitchen hell.

On Labor Day weekend, I peeled the skin off my fingers instead of apples and suffered a burn bad enough to land me in the emergency room. The doctor turned out to be one of my customers.

"I know you," he said, reviewing my chart. "Grrreat Bordelaise sauce," he growled like Tony the Frosted Flakes Tiger as he bandaged my right hand.

In our upstairs apartment, I wept in bed.

"You are needing help, Kitchie. You have started us. But now we must hire *professionals*."

I was too tired to be offended.

And so by autumn we had hired our first professional, the meanest cook in America, Able Cane, from Georgia. On the outside he looked like a Georgia cracker. On the inside he was a Georgia cracker, only smart. Blood smart. Able was nasty enough to disembowel people, but, luckily for the human race, he had decided to confine his cruelty to chickens and lambs. Aside from being one of the best cooks I had ever met, Able was also the meanest.

Able had grown up in a small town in rural Georgia where his father had designed airplane engines for the military and his mother had been the town librarian. His parents had expected Able to go on through college.

"Wanted me to get a million degrees and do something pro-*fesh*ional, and that rhymes with con-*fesh*ional, but I don't be-lieve in church, and I don't believe in school. I din't want to be no goddamn paper jerk so I lit off to New York City to do my own thing, love power and all that garbage."

Able was consistent in that he despised everything, even the things he believed in. At the time he came to work for us, he was camping out with his wife and two babies on Rivington Street in a building abandoned by the landlord, given up for lost by the city. He was part of a renegade commune of urban homesteaders, and he hoped one day to sell his squatter's shares in the resuscitated building and make a profit.

"Out of absolutely nothing, and that's the goddamn beauty of it." Foodwise, Able found this same value in offal and loved nothing better than showing a big profit off a piece of flesh no-body in their right mind would want to eat, like deep-fried brains in rhubarb beurre blanc, his signature dish.

With the exception of the white, double-buttoned chef's jacket, Able eschewed the rest of the standard kitchen uniform of checkered pants and toque. Instead he wore army fatigues and a baseball hat which hid his marine-regulation crew cut which he happily referred to as his "baldy bean."

"This way," he explained, "I know any goddamn hair in the food ain't mine."

He came to his job interview chewing on a toothpick. Able had worked at some of the best places in town but always as an underling cook, never as a chef in charge. Ralph the dog, pres-ent at all interviews, liked Able immediately. But then, Ralph also liked toilet bowls.

"I could get used to it here," he said. "I like you two, and I see this here as a place I can kind of spread out in, if you know what I mean."

Able was as uncompromising about food as he was about everything else. He took no short cuts; he researched his dishes and ideas, all of which came with histories and pedigrees.

His first night at Kittridge's, we worked side by side at the stove. At one point, watching me sauté, he burst out with, "Woman, don't you know how to hold a sauce pan?" He took the pan and showed me my mistake. At the end of the evening he said, "Well, you're a good cook, but you're no damn good at service."

"Who asked you?"

"Hell, you want the value of my experience, don't you? It's why you hired me, ain't that true? You don't let go of plates, and you ain't quick enough. Looka here, I see you *are* a fine baker. Why don't you concentrate on that and let me do this stuff?"

"In other words, move over."

"Yep," he smiled, happy I'd gotten the point so quickly. "Something like that."

He rode me whenever I made a mistake. "Well, there she goes again, the sister with the golden touch."

"This Able," said Gunnar one evening after service, "he is good in the kitchen but he is very mean guy. You are sure you want to continue with him?"

Able had begun to take over many of my jobs, and my work life was significantly less burdened and crazed.

"Are the customers happy with the food?"

"Sure. Is coming out on time, nobody waits anymore, taste is fine, more compliments than ever."

"That's all that's important. Able's okay in his disgusting kind of way."

"Okay," said Gunnar reluctantly. "But time to get rid of him is now, early before he settles in comfortable. Time to say something is soon, please, Kitchie."

"Oh, my God," Rayburn Billy gasped. "White trash. And it's cooking in your kitchen. Down West Virginia we know a thing or two about crackers. They may sound stupid," he explained, "but they're smart right down to their bones. You sure you want that viper in your kitchen?"

Why didn't I fire him? Why did I continue to work with such a smart ass? First of all, he was very good, and we were very busy. Delivering the goods was all I could really think of just then. Besides, our staff grew larger and his jokes were no longer at my expense.

By November, we had hired Danny Boy. He came to Kittridge's after traveling around Europe, having eaten and drunk everything in sight, studying food and working in kitchens wherever he could. In comparison to Able's downright meanness, Danny Boy was sincerity itself. The son of a successful New Jersey lawyer, Danny came from a long line of liberals, and instead of going to college, he had taken a rebellious toot through Europe. He had caught up with himself in France where, as he told us on his interview, he discovered that "the real me loved food." Unschooled in anything else, cooking was Danny Boy's path to self-revelation. He referred to his "cuisine" with mawkish sincerity, but he had a good, strong back and completed whatever task he was given. He was, in the words of the profession, a workhorse.

Danny was also a crier, a real bawler. A good-looking brussels sprout could move Danny to tears. "I'm into the poetry of food." Like Able, Danny Boy had a hobby, but instead of abandoned buildings, Danny attended a New Age bioenergetic self-help group whose members believed in confrontational therapy. Naturally, Danny Boy considered working under Able's tutelage a great opportunity for self-growth; apparently, getting beaten up by a bigger, meaner cook was the same thing as learning something worth knowing.

As gaunt, sinewy and fair as Able was, Danny Boy was squat, dark and hairy. Able approved of hiring Danny Boy.

"He's a bull, all right. Perfect for lifting all those goddamn stock pots." I agreed with Able, as heaving fifty pounds of soup was not my idea of a good time either. As an extra bonus, Danny was a whiz at butchering; he knew his meats and knives. But strong as he was, he was without discipline. Danny Boy couldn't make the same dish the same way twice. He was always wanting to be *creative*.

"Don't you get it, boy? This is about making the same thing the same way fourteen hundred times. We are not talking sparks of inspiration here, boy." Able shook his head.

Danny Boy wanted desperately to make specials, but whatever he made was worse than what he had made before: heavy-handed, angst-laden food, like his venison ragout with tree ears, corn and sauerkraut dumplings. Danny Boy would proudly present a new dish for Able to taste, and Able would first push it around with a fork, suspiciously, looking to uncover something offensive, the way children do when given something new to taste.

"Hey, old buddy," Able would snarl, "this thing is brown, brown, brown. Heavy brown. All your food is brown. Don't you know no other color? You come looka here at this plate you just gave me and tell me why such a nice New Jersey boy like you is always cooking with shit?"

There was something in that, I supposed. Danny Boy had that two year old's fixation with food mess. Stir it, rub it into mishmash, smear it on your hands, roll it around in flour, fry it, stick on a radicchio leaf, and call it a masterpiece. Any Freudian worth his salt would have said that Danny was the prime example of someone whose parents had applauded him too loudly during his early toilet-training efforts. Danny Boy was born to want confirmation from Able, who was born never to give it. Not that Able didn't take Danny Boy under his wing.

"First of all, you asshole," he drilled, "you report to work with a notebook and write your recipes down."

"I'm an instinctive cook."

"Carve 'em in stone, jerkoff, and carry 'em with you to your next job. It ain't your good looks that make you valuable, Bud, it's that little black book."

Danny continued to show Able his newest ideas for specials. It was unanimous, none of us liked what Danny cooked. We hardly ever let him run a special, yet he kept on coming up with them, from pickled pig ears couscous to steak barbecued in egg yolk and pimento sauce.

"You stay up at night just thinking of these things, Boy?"

Danny uncovered a dish of skate wrapped in kale and powdered mushrooms.

"Boy, this food is frightening."

Danny's eyes welled up.

"You got a thing for nasty-ugly or what? Don't you never think green or white?"

"Well, my purees are very colorful—"

"That squishy shit?" Able said disgustedly. "You're back in that outhouse again, brother. Liven up yourself, heaven's sake."

By December there was one more addition to the kitchen staff, Wasabe, a Japanese cook whose respectful Eastern manners put the two other cooks to shame. Wasabe bowed whenever Gunnar or I walked in the room. He never answered back, and when he wasn't bowing he was smiling. His English was poor, but his work was perfect. He could sculpt a radish like Brancusi.

Danny Boy now directed his best efforts towards Wasabe and showed all his turned vegetables to him. Bows and grunts were Wasabe's way of criticizing poor Danny Boy's best efforts.

"In my country, master beats cook for such work," Wasabe offered sternly with a polite bow and a knowing raise of the eyebrows.

As Danny Boy would skulk away to his corner of the prep table, Able would approve by repeating his favorite one-liner to Wasabe. "DWC, good buddy, DWC. Death of Western Civilization."

Wasabe would grunt like a samurai and shake his head.

"And we'll all be better off for it, too, good buddy," Able would add. "Personally, I can't wait."

Wasabe was the only exemplary in the kitchen. He alone kept peace in the kitchen because they all wanted to learn his exquisite techniques. "In my country," Wasabe would begin politely with a bow as the boys gathered around him while he demonstrated how to carve a turnip into a six-foot see-though strip, "master charges one hundred dollars to teach this."

Valentine was the last cook to be hired. Valentine of the

mango ice cream, the crispy fried noodles, the shrimp wrapped in banana leaves.

Valentine had grown up on a rice farm in Luzon, the central Philippines. He loved the harvest, the watery fields between his toes, the long reeds in his hands. He wanted to be a farmer and work the land, but to please his father he had studied economics instead. While studying at the university, Valentine became a political organizer. After a brief but humiliating imprisonment, he fled his country to finish his studies in America. He had learned to cook from his mother, and while he pursued his doctorate, he supported himself by working in restaurants. He was dexterous with a knife, and by the time he had earned his doctorate, he was a line cook in Boston.

Valentine accepted a teaching job at a private college on the east coast. During his classes his thoughts would drift away from Marx to plump chicken legs stuffed with chevre and green curry. Like a culinary Jekyll and Hyde, he led two lives, teaching by day and cooking by night. Soon enough, an over-tired Valentine got into a terrible row with his department chairman who did not rehire him for the following term. Valentine took a job in one of Philadelphia's best restaurants where, in time, he became sous-chef. He met his future wife, the daughter of a wealthy diplomat, who was as charming as Valentine was abrasive. Together, they worked for Filipino civil rights, but where his wife was a cool-headed, effective organizer, the temperamental Valentine fell into heated debates. Soon he cooked for rallies but did not go to them. With more time to concentrate on his career, he outgrew the Philadelphia job and he and Mary-Rose moved to New York where her father bought them a brownstone in Brooklyn.

Valentine seemed determined to bring politics into the kitchen. The world of socioeconomic injustice became part of everyday chitchat as he lectured us on welfare reform, immigration policies, world hunger while we prepared food. Able balked, knowing that Valentine had become very American in his tastes. His home's expensive furnishings might have been explained by his wife's money, but Valentine's kitchen was equipped with every up-to-date gadget and machine from bread baker to pasta maker. He relished his electric one-egg whisk with the perverse humor of a critic, the avid curiosity of a foreigner, and, as Able knew, with the pride of an owner.

"You ain't exactly cooking for the pro-lo-tear-iat here, Val. Now, that's a natural-born fact you got to get yourself used to, old buddy." In his snide way, Able had meant to be sympathetic, even concerned, but as usual he hit upon a painful nerve.

Whenever Valentine got mad, his broad face grew red, his nostrils flared like a wild horse angrily snorting at its bridle. He turned to the stove, shaking a fry pan full of innocent little onions caramelizing in sugar back and forth over the flames. Shake and snort, shake and snort. Valentine threw his cleaver down with enough force to crack the butcher block.

Valentine's temper, Able's cruelty, Danny Boy's lack of talent, Wasabe's superiority. There were good reasons to fire each one, but there were better reasons to keep them. With this culinary Marx Brothers in place, service went smoothly, even as the numbers of customers slowly but steadily increased. My professional experience amounted to a few months of selling sandwiches on the street, and though I couldn't teach them any kitchen tricks they didn't already know, I could teach them about taste. I had learned a great deal working in the Baron's kitchen, gussying up regional vittles in preparation for his *Wake Up, America* program. The Baron, a fastidious researcher, was in the business of popularizing every dish we cooked. I was also a graduate of Jenks and Wolenska's Thursday Tasters where careful reading of the J&W *Weekly Tum* had revealed everything anyone would want to know about up-and-coming food trends.

The food world, such as it was, had parallels to the art world. Or, as Lilly said at cocktail parties, selling art was no different than selling brassieres. It was all a matter of recognizing the it of now. It was all a matter of following the changing eye. Putting in front of it what it wanted to see next, putting on the tongue the flavors it wanted to taste next. Thanks to Lilly, I understood how to spot a trend and sell it better than anyone who worked for me. That was what I gave the kitchen boys, and even Able was glad to follow along.

"Girl," he would say after I critiqued his cooking, "if I didn't know you better, I'd have to say you know what you want."

American food, as I saw it, was as much about who was in my kitchen as anything else. We'd start with a southern dish, fried chicken or pan-blackened fish, which Able would perfect. Wasabe would take it over, adding a daikon or seaweed salad. Valentine would add a package of rice wrapped in banana leaves, and Danny Boy, whose greatest strength besides his back was his ability to cook on the line under pressure, would execute the dish faithfully at the stove during service. Together we made an ethnic amalgam that was as American as shoofly pie.

In this way, I directed the kitchen, and while Able, Danny, Wasabe and Valentine took on more of the nighttime work of service, I began to learn how to run the front of the house. The idea of spending time in the dining room had been rolling around in my head for a while, but it was something Gunnar said one night as we were closing up that convinced me. The waiters were still wiping down tables when Gunnar pulled me into our office and closed the door.

"Leesen, Kitchie," he said conspiratorially. "You are boss now. Is your name on canopy, no?" Gunnar was warming up for the pitch.

"You are boss and boss can work anywhere, right?" He warmed a brandy with his hands and puffed slowly on his cigar. "You can learn whole business, not just kitchen. Front and back. Is best to know everything. Then you not gonna need nobody but you self. We gonna learn, learn from all these smart guys we hire. Then we both gonna know our business better than anyone." In Finnish, he mumbled one of his mother's favorite sayings, something about a bull getting pulled around by the ring in his nose. He put a clenched fist to his mouth and bit his thumbnail. "Best way to guarantee, how you say, guard safe what we have here is to learn about business from all angles. Is best way." He blew some rings, doused some ash, and sat up straight. "Best way," he said again, decisively. "What you think?"

Looking at the restaurant as a business instead of a love-child could do me no harm. It could only put me in a stronger position to know the overall picture of how my business worked. It was true that I preferred making food to selling it; it was also obvious that in a business with so many details, the more I could control, the better off I would be. Thoughts of my little country diner floated into my consciousness: soups, fresh-baked breads, hand-painted signs I'd tack up above the counter so that the trickle of customers in their leatherette booths would smile as they read. . . .

The kitchen boys warmed to the idea that I was spending some of my time out front. Wasabe was the most politic. "Woman makes egg, man cooks it." He smiled at me cryptically and bowed.

Nine

Everything I needed to know about restaurant dining rooms I learned from Harmon Borsch. Harmon, a recent college graduate, had worked his way through college selling bagels on campus during the mornings and bartending at the local pub at night. Along the way, he had acquired a taste for expensive Burgundy and decided to become a sommelier. He was short, his teeth were crooked, and his nose was too big. Harmon had the face of a shlub, the soul of a bootlegger and the charm of an oil drum. He was only too glad to train me because any night I ran the front, he would talk vintages with the customers. Harmon could sell water as long as it was in a green Bordeaux bottle.

Getting along with customers was a survival tactic in this business, and I was taking lessons from a master. "They want to think you're having a party, so let them. Now, a lot of people find your kind of shyness charming. Okay, there's no accounting for taste but remember, all they want is a little *feel-good*. It's part of what they're paying for. So be nice. Relax. You don't have to go to bed with them.

"And smile at them, Kitchie. Smile like you mean it. It's your job to make them feel comfortable. Unless, of course, they're rich, in which case just follow *their* lead and remember, sincere in-gratiation is your best shot. That, and the ability to become invisible while you're standing at the table waiting for them to order."

"How do you smile and bow and stay out of the way?" I asked, admiring his style for seeming to disappear, only to appear again in an instant when summoned by the customer.

"Like rubbing your stomach and patting your head at the same time?" he asked, grinning. "Learn to grovel," he advised me. "Welcome to the hospitality industry."

While I was learning how to fold napkins, make a margarita, and work the room, Gunnar was learning how to get along in the kitchen. He still couldn't tell a peach from a tennis ball, but he had learned all the stations and knew something about ordering, scheduling, and maintaining the kitchen's organization. Danny Boy was teaching him how to sauté, and under Wasabe's watchful eye, he was learning how to carve vegetables for garnishes. When, with Valentine's help, he tried his hand at a few side dishes, leaning towards root vegetables and Scandinavian favorites, even Able found a few words of encouragement.

"You curb those cabbage-stuffing, potato-boiling Russkie impulses, boy, and you'll be all right, I guess."

Maybe it was the inevitable course of our relationship, and not just because we were in danger of disappearing into our creation, but the nature of our lovemaking had changed. Up to now, there had been a natural giving and taking, an uncomplicated slipping into one another. Now, it was the language of profit that we whispered into each other's ears, not love. Our most intimate moments began to sound like we were ordering off a menu. Touch me here. Squeeze me there, pull, lick, bite. Turn around, get on your knees. Do it harder. Occasionally we made love, but most times we had sex. We had entered into that sexual zone of fulfilling each other's needs. How do you want it? Where do you want me to put it? Somehow, disrobing our fantasies had stripped our lovemaking, turned it stark and standard. I missed the froufrou and the tender seductions.

After every sexual spree, instead of enjoying the afterglow, I'd leave our bed and descend quietly to Kittridge's to make sure the stoves were off and the walk-in closed. Everything was tucked in for the night except me. When I returned to bed, Gunnar would whisper, "Hey, you are scared? Work, love, everyone is scared. Come here, I gonna rub your back." We'd return to that libidinous wish list. He would have liked nothing more than to grant me a few of my wishes. I just didn't seem to have any left.

"What do you want me to do to you? You would like to suck me, maybe?" he would ask kindly, as though this would fix things. What did I know about gender logic? Romance made a woman soft, pliant and wet. It made a man hard. Close to climax, Gunnar would suck in his breath, savoring his sensation, and he would whisper, "Come to papa, baby, come to papa." Were we making love or shooting craps? Were those his balls I fondled or a pair of dice?

Gunnar had begun to search food sections of daily newspapers for mention of our name, lusting after reviews. "Why we are not getting reviewed? How come they don't know we here?" He took this oversight as a personal affront and seemed genuinely hurt. While Gunnar schemed for ways to put us on the city's culinary map by making new friends and influencing new people, I tried to stay in touch with our old friends.

Rayburn Billy came to dinner as a paying customer, and he always brought other interns. He and Harmon liked to talk wine, and Billy always bought an expensive bottle. Ginger was busy with social-work school but stopped by the bar to tell me her marriage had finally collapsed. "He kept the power tools, and I got a big box of wooden yo-yos and the apartment," she explained. We catered Dolores' birthday party, thrown for her by her agent who ordered a cake in the shape of two breasts. Frenchie, who was ending a tour with The Babes, sent postcards from San Diego. No message, just his signature: your friend, Frenchie. Wally was painting again and very prolific. He had produced thirty canvases in one month, all of Fatima.

"Naked, of course," he explained over the telephone. "It took me thirty pictures, but I finally got what I wanted."

"And Fatima?" I asked.

"She wants to marry me. She can afford it too. Her uncle wants to set her up with one of his pushcarts, selling falafels in Brooklyn."

Compared to our increasingly complicated life downstairs, our life upstairs had a certain spiritual simplicity. We had neither the time nor the imagination to shape our apartment into a home. Our days were spent working in the richly cluttered atmosphere of the restaurant, our nights at home were spent in a bare-bones habitat. Roving sets of Kittridge's wine glasses, coffee cups and Perrier bottles made their way up and down, passing between the borders of our restaurant, that land of good and plenty, and our apartment, a poor, underdeveloped nation by comparison.

We owned a rocking chair, a table and a futon on the floor which doubled for a couch. I kept my clothes in two plastic milk crates. A jumble of cardboard boxes lined the walls, filled with unexamined debris. Our bathroom towels didn't match, our oven didn't work. Our mini refrigerator was so frozen over, there wasn't enough room to wedge in a Popsicle. Was there a dining table in our future? Matching couch and armchair? I had lied to our cleaning woman, a devout Jehovah's Witness, promising that one day in this domestic desert there would be real furniture to clean. But all I managed was to get our mattress off the floor onto a box spring, which at least gave Ruth something to sweep under.

My mother began to show up for dinner once a week. She liked to sit at the bar with her cronies, slowly sipping wine spritzers. Lilly had started thinking of the restaurant differently. The Weggs and the von Schornbergs had asked her to arrange a table for four on a Saturday night and had even written her thank-you notes when she had done so. Her acquaintances spoke about the dishes they'd had at Kittridge's with the same importance reserved for discussing art. My mother Lilly had begun to reconsider. Perhaps a restaurant was a kind of performance medium? Lilly and I agreed on one thing: If cooking was an art, it was the only one that was eaten.

When I was growing up, the window shade in my mother's kitchen had always been drawn at half mast. The soulless Caloric was used to defrost, not cook. Our refrigerator was chronically barren; even the ice cube trays were empty. The metal dining table, not considered important enough to merit its own room, was relegated to the dimly lit foyer. There, between the two coat closets, Toddy, my old babysitter, fed me Swanson TV dinners, still frozen at the heart. My parents worked late every night, and we rarely ate together. Instead, I had my meals in solitude. Out of loneliness, then, I discovered that mashed potatoes could become volcanoes about to erupt with molten gravy, and french fries the soldiers with whom I planned revolts.

One day, troubled by our lack of reviews, Gunnar announced he was interviewing publicists. Our conversation about hiring a public relations firm took place all day, trailing behind everything else we did, like a child's blanky. Work left us no time to speak privately, so we spoke when we could, picking up the threads of our conversation while checking in meat deliveries, the linen order, or while the produce truck unloaded. I had become more adamant as the day had worn on, while Gunnar turned peevish, frustrated with what he perceived as my complacency. The debate crawled into bed with us that night.

"I don't understand you sometimes, Gunnar. It's hard to keep up with things as it is. When will enough be enough? When we build Kittridge's Two? Three? Four? Exactly what is it you want?"

He beat his pillow into shape, an old goose-down his mother had sent with him to America, without which it was impossible for him to fall asleep. He pounded his pillow, that old soft thing, that substitute for safety. He spoke from an inner battleground.

"What do I want? What do I *want*? Just I want to *survive*. That's all. Just I want to be in goddamn business when shit-fuck dust settles after bullshit is over. *I want to be here*," he said, angrily hammering his pillow with every word. Then he turned his back on me and went to sleep.

The next morning I awoke to find him sitting up in bed, the covers thrown carelessly over his naked lap. I could see he wanted to make up, which, of course, meant getting his way.

"Just because Monday is busy does not mean Tuesday gonna make money too." He pleaded with me to see the light. "Is good business sense. Public relations firm is logical next step."

Gunnar was always taking Next Steps, while I was getting ready to Settle In.

"Can't we just work with what we've got?"

"This is bad attitude, Kitchie," he warned.

"Why? We've got a good business. Why don't you leave it alone for a while and just let things be?" I couldn't understand Gunnar's propensity for getting bigger. These days, I switched between front and back of the house so many times in a single day that I seemed to be whirling around in a perpetual revolving door.

"I want a chance to catch up," I explained.

"Time to catch up is when you dead. In life is always time to move on."

"I know how you're thinking," I accused him. "I know what you want. Kittridge's East Coast, Kittridge's West Coast, Kittridge's in fucking Chicago."

"Now you talking. Is right time for PR guy."

My dream restaurant was fading fast. A big lawn, a simple house, brown mugs, a long counter, donuts and muffins, funny names for the sandwiches. . . .

"Hey, you are regretting something? Is something we need to talk about?"

The strong hand around my waist, pulling me to him, the warmth of his breath, those sweet Lapland kisses. I stroked his curly hair, so full of spiraling energy.

"Why don't we ever take a vacation?"

"Okay. Next year, palm trees. First we are hiring public relations person."

We were always doing something first.

"Newspapers gonna know we here, they will review. Then we gonna get on big success road, lots of money."

Our success hung in the air like electricity, an element so pure he could taste it; this was the food of Gunnar's existence. He pulled me onto his lap and rocked me gently from side to side, kissing me. The fear of failure fell away from my body.

"We cannot fail. Is not question of luck, but performance. Like betting on right horse," he murmured as though he were giving me a science lesson. "You are making good cooking. I am making good money. Together we—" He searched for the right American word. "Click. You and me, Kitchie, we click."

His optimism washed over me like a rolling sea. I hoped we wouldn't drown. Like any surfer, I was a sucker for a wave, even if I didn't trust the ride.

Ten

For Gunnar, survival meant hiring a food yenta, someone who liked to eat and talk to someone else who liked to eat and talk and so on down the chain of eaters and talkers. Gunnar found his food yenta in Tom Bolognese. Tom had single-handedly engineered the promotion of the kiwi in the U.S. and was legendary for his contacts with mega food companies, those cereal producers who had produced half the world's frozen food. Tom promised us our personal hunk of Hollywood as we signed his contract on the dotted line: our recipes published in *Gourmet*, a restaurateur's version of immortality.

The long promotional arm of Bolognese & Bolognese worked best in food campaigns that were sponsored by corporate representational bodies such as The Rice Association. The Ricers would sponsor a contest and hire a panel of cooks and food journalists from all over the country who would mull over thousands of recipes submitted by amateur cooks and high school home economics majors. Submissions consisted of the kind of "new and creative ideas" that typically ended up on the back of every box of, say, Insta-Rice. The panel considered recipes for rice-sagna, rice-eroles, and rice-a-ritters. The winner would receive a trip to Brazil or a college scholarship, the awards to be presented at a luncheon held at a hot new restaurant in a major city to which every important food journalist in the country was invited. The bigger the corporation, the more journalists came. Cocktails were served, writers and editors chatted with old friends in the business, and the winning entry was served. Food reporters were expected to take an admiring, though understandably small, bite of their lunch. After a rice appetizer, rice entree and rice dessert, a speech would be made by a company executive who sank the story hook which would find its way through press releases into the Associated Press and end up in local and national food columns. A gift was given to the reporters upon their leaving (Limoges rice bowls, key chains shaped like mini chop sticks). Across the capital cities of America, this was how food was sold, and through Gunnar's persistence, Kittridge's was now, at last, a player of this inner circle of promotion and self-promotion.

The Bolognese plan for Kittridge's involved boosting our image to national star status. With this end in mind, Tom had invited us to the American Cold Cut Cornucopia in San Francisco. We would be Demonstrator Chefs and all our expenses would be paid by the Cold Cut Committee of the American Cold Cut Foundation. The Cornucopia was our first chance to taste serious national media blitzkrieg.

"You'll be in the hands of complete professionals. What you'll learn about PR will be invaluable," promised Tom.

The Cold Cut Committee sent us a colorful poster depicting over fifty varieties of luncheon meat. Along with the poster came an official letter explaining that Kittridge's was to present three original recipes using hot dogs, ham butt and low-fat turkey roll. There were to be two days of panels and lectures, and we would be interviewed by syndicated journalists on a dinner cruise around San Francisco Bay which featured the Demonstrator Chefs' original cold cut dishes.

"But we never cook hot dogs. Or ham butt," I objected.

"Could have been worse," Gunnar pointed to the list of other Demonstrator Chefs. "One poor guy is cooking with head cheese."

Our hotel in San Francisco had glass walls, glass elevators, and even the concierge's desk shone like crystal. The porter in spats and bowler hat carried our bags up to our room as live music rose up the central court through all the corridors and oozed underneath the doors of the suites like musical goo. This was the kind of place my mother would have hated, but Gunnar was enjoying it all, right down to the bellboy's golden epaulets. He loved the bad music, the grandiose architecture, the excessive luxury. His pleasure with all this was not to be taken lightly; he considered being here an achievement. The fact that it would be short-lived made him want to savor every moment in this fishbowl.

Our room was glass on two sides. We looked over the Bay and watched the lights of San Francisco start to twinkle. There was even a large bouquet of roses on our coffee table. "Here's to fun and profit. Glad to have you aboard the good ship Cold Cuts. Best Wishes from the Cornucopia Committee!"

We smelled the roses, kissed, and savored the view. Who could resist the romance of this moment? The pleasure of darkening sky, moonlit water and the sparkling lights surrounding the bay soon turned into stimuli for touching and feeling each other's bodies. Stars and champagne added to our ardor as we tongue-kissed and took each other's clothes off. We hobbled, kissed, hobbled, kissed, to the bed. It seemed we were fucking not just each other but our success. We were making love not just to each other's bodies but to what they had accomplished. Proud of how well we fit together, pulled together, like two draft horses, a working team plowing the field. God help us, we were in love with our potential.

"You are so beautiful. I love you face, you hair, you eyes. I love you. I love what you do. I love what we doing together. I love *us*."

I couldn't help laughing. The room was so ugly, and Gunnar was so corny.

"Why you are laughing? I must say this to you. I owe you. Without you, what would I be selling?"

I remembered how I had once thought he was a southern boy, American down to his jeans.

"You would have been selling *something*," I assured him. "You were born to make money. You *like* all this."

"And you do not?"

"Not as much as you do. I just wanted to *do* something I loved."

"And now?"

My little country diner hovered above the bed, plastic pink flamingoes set up on the lawn, a line out the door, waiting for brunch. . . .

"Now I'm *with* someone I love."

Cocktails Friday night at 8:00 P.M. in the Blue Ballroom treated us to tables decorated with ice sculptures and cornucopia baskets overflowing with fruits, rolls, chocolates, cookies and, of course, cold cuts of every imaginable shape and size. The

Demonstrator Chefs mingled with famous food stars and compared notes. Handsome Michael O'Sullivan, the Jack Nicholson of the food world, was there with his slicked-back hair, looking more like a movie star than a chef. Lauren Dime was showing off the latest gadget she'd found while on tour in Japan. Jerry Newman shared his brilliant marketing techniques while he grabbed necks and rubbed backs like a coach at a swim meet. But the eyes and the snapping cameras were on Dimitri Mozart who, the month before, had posed naked in the centerfold of an international cook's magazine. Dimitri wouldn't be staying for the whole Cornucopia, he explained, since he was just passing through on his way to opening a new Dimitri's in L.A.

Stately Millicent Nottingham, doyenne of American food and author of several encyclopedic cooking volumes, shook our hand as a beaming Tom Bolognese took us around and introduced us. Nobody here knew from plain food. There was a woman who grew organic tarragon, a man who raised lamb by day and captained a tugboat by night, a tall, spooky Oregonian with skin the color of dusty chanterelles who picked wild mushrooms, and a New Age farmer who named his farm after a T.S. Eliot poem who had changed the color of carrots and the size of zucchini. We gathered around a straw cornucopia for photographs. We entertained each other with stories about New Zealand razor clams and Vancouver scallops. The food intelligentsia had an eccentric sweetness. We pitched our products to each other over cocktails, and the evening took on a self-congratulatory tone.

Saturday morning after our breakfast of coffee and mini danish, we got right down to business. The Cold Cut Committee had hired Marti Snidelman, vice president of Snidelman and

Snidelman Communications, to prepare the Demonstrator Chefs for the interviews that would take place on the twilight cruise around San Francisco. The CCC expected the press to be antagonistic to beef and nitrates, and Marti was a specialist at training media naifs to field hostile questions. She gave us basic training dealing with the Press Cong. War was hell as Marti primed us for a belligerent media by putting us through tough-love interviews taped and replayed for our own good.

"Okay, what do you know about olive loaf?" barked Marti.

"Is good on bread with mayonnaise?" answered Gunnar. I fared no better.

"Suppose a reporter tastes your deviled ham and says, 'Doesn't this have a lot of sodium?' So you say—"

"So I say, 'Yes, it does.'"

It became obvious that neither Gunnar nor I were naturally gifted when it came to discussing shelf life with reporters. Gunnar was a more willing student, whereas I worried I would be asked to move my lips, but not to sing. Of all the Demonstrator Chefs, Dixon Belvedere best represented bologna and salami. Dixon, with his soft, uninspired face, big hands and thick fingers, could look straight into the camera as Marti threw him jibe after jibe, and lie.

"There is nothing more wholesome than one of these great-looking keel-bah-sees." He held up a string of the fat sausages. "We smoke our own and our customers come back for more!" He walked through a simple recipe and ended with, "Mmm mmm. Now that's good eating, and it won't break your piggy bank."

Marti threw him a jibe. "Looks like you eat plenty of your mistakes, Dix—"

Dixon laughed good-naturedly. "Yes ma'am, and I eat plenty of the good stuff too."

Marti congratulated him with a stop-the-press flourish. Dixon, that robust progenitor of Creole cooking, knew how to give cold cuts his all. By the time the afternoon of rehearsed interviews was over, he had managed to tell an imaginary hostile press that nitrates were not only American, they were Godsent.

A firm called The Casual Caterer had been hired to prepared our recipes for the evening's boat ride around the bay, but somehow The Casual Caterer had missed the whole point of the job. Instead of wrapping chef Annie Delgado's quail in bacon, they stuck the bacon inside the bird, where it couldn't be seen. They had left out the salami in sullen Rachel Binkner's crawfish casserole.

"Jesu Christo, they change our ham recipe too. Was bad enough but now is tasting like brown paper bag." They had left out the brandy in our deviled ham butt pâté. The only dish that came out all right was Dixon Belvedere's Heartland Gumbo.

"Indestructible," smiled a proud Dixon.

We all watched as Marti lambasted The Casual Caterer.

"Hey, very excellent example of hostile interview," whispered Gunnar as we watched and listened to Marti plough down the catering staff. "Too bad we are missing video camera."

The Cornucopia brochure had described the evening boat ride as "a culinary tour around sparkling San Francisco Bay." The "*Ship of Foods*," as one newspaper had heralded it, set sail just before sunset. There was a festive atmosphere as the boat took off and left the dock. Guests stood around with glasses of wine and champagne. Cocktail napkins slipped from their hands and littered the floor of the old cruiser like snow. Everyone wore a name tag above his or her heart.

The water lapped peacefully against the side of the boat as the chefs stood behind long serving tables stationed around the deck. They were hard at work slicing, cutting, ladling sauces over food they were not happy with. Except for Dixon, who was busy telling a reporter about his croissant maker, praline-manufacturing machine, and his computer expeditor system.

"Food comes out of our kitchen so fast, we're ready to feed the next century."

As I ate his gumbo, which was every bit as bad as our ham butt pâté, Dixon smiled at me.

"Y'all bring me a hunk of that fine ham spread of yours, you hear?"

People were eating all over the place, resting their wine glasses on any available ledge. They tasted off each other's plates and reviewed: more salt, less salt, what was that herb? Critics and food writers from both coasts were stuffing their faces full of cold cuts. Was the Cornucopia a true educational force in American food, as the CCC president had said in a welcome speech at the beginning of the cruise?

That's what Nancy Greene, syndicated food journalist, wanted to know too. There was pure ambulance chaser coursing through Nancy's veins. It was hard to believe such a hard-nosed reporter was more interested in cooks than criminals, but food was her beat, and she could spend hours talking about roast vegetables. Nancy didn't have a lot of time, so you answered her questions directly and quickly. You gave Nancy the story she was looking for, or you hid from her. You didn't change the subject or compliment her dress. I watched her bend over the dish she was eating. Her black hair fell over one side of her face. She pushed it aside with her long fingers. She looked up like the instinctive media animal she was and caught me just as I was looking away to avoid her. She sidled up close.

"This Cornucopia thing been your cup of tea?"

I took too long to answer so she answered for me.

"Gunnar takes to flashbulbs like a fish to water."

"He likes attention," I smiled uncomfortably. Marti had taught Gunnar well.

"They love the Balkan angle," she said as we both watched the reporters cluster around him a few feet away. "That communist stuff just slays them. And then of course he's half Scandinavian, so that clinches it. Golden boy. Any plans for posing for the cooks' calendar?"

"Which one is that?" I asked, confused by the many offers that had come to us lately via Tom Bolognese.

"Naked buns, just a hint of groin and belly hair. Thunder Bay Beer. You know," she sang the jingle quickly, "'Get A Load of the Head on This One.'"

"Guess I haven't heard it."

"So, are you jealous?" Nancy looked me dead center in the eyes.

"Not about the naked buns," was about all I could think to say.

We both watched as a group of three reporters clustered around Gunnar. They were less belligerent about nitrates and more interested in the story of Gunnar's immigration.

"So after you escaped the Iron Curtain—" they asked.

"Tell us about the years eating sardines and flatbread—"

"Were you always interested in cooking?"

"Where did you study?"

"I learn everything from Kitchie," he said, looking in my direction. "She is real inspiration behind our restaurant." He motioned for me to come join him, but I shook my head. I motioned that I was deep in the conversation pit with Nancy.

"For an up-and-coming press junkie, he's loyal, I'll give you that," said Nancy.

We were joined by the reporters who had finished interviewing Gunnar and had worked their way over to where Nancy and I were standing.

"Got the next Dimitri Mozart over there, a real comer." A reporter shook my hand. "You guys married or just friends or a team or what?"

Nancy looked at me closely.

"Lovers and Partners."

"Great answer. Can't use it, but I love it anyway."

"It's the name of our next cafe," I said.

"You don't say?"

"Cappuccino and desserts only. Nothing too serious, sweets only. The food of love. We're calling it unbetrothed cuisine."

Nancy gave me a long look and scraped her plate. "Honey, you can really get going once you start," she said and went off to muckrake with someone else.

If I was jealous, I was also relieved that Gunnar was taking care of this part of the job. He invited attention and held it; he pleased people, gave them what they wanted with ease. Without him, there would be no flashbulbs. I supposed I was jealous of the same things I loved about him.

As we cruised back into the harbor at the end of the evening, Marti was handing out postcard-size ballots that read:

Star light star bright
Lots of stars on board tonight
So vote the dish
That's most dee-lish!

Underneath this was a list of all the dishes tasted on board, with little boxes next to them so that reporters could cast their votes. It had never occurred to me that cooking was a competitive sport.

We rode the glass elevator to our glass-walled room one last transparent time before we left San Francisco, and as it ascended to the twelfth floor and hovered over the central court of the hotel, I felt we had been swallowed by a robot in a sci-fi movie. We took the red-eye home that night and returned to Kittridge's and to our less than glittering digs.

Was I culinary madonna or culinary whore? I never had time to figure it out because the offers came so fast. For months after the Cold Cut Cornucopia symposium, Mega Food was on the march. The Cheese Board had us pose with cows while sitting on a three-foot hunk of Emmentaler. The New Zealand Farm Board had us wear crowns of frozen baby lamb chops. We hosted Uncle Mike's Kasha Cook-Off, and Aunt Bet's Barley Bake-Off for which, at our insistence, Valentine had reluctantly invented such politically incorrect dishes as Filipino Adobong Kasha.

Some campaigns had morally complicated plots. According to Bolognese & Bolognese's marketing polls, their client, Kentucky Bourbon, had sent more teenage heads into toilets than any other alcoholic drink in America. Memories of bad hangovers kept teen drinkers from touching the stuff as adults, so Kittridge's was hired to spearhead the new cook-with-Kentucky-Bourbon campaign kick-off, featuring bourbon soup, bourbon chicken, bourbon race-track cake decorated with chocolate horses. Our wait staff wore jockey uniforms and handed departing journalists bottles of thirty-year-old killer bourbon.

Heightened political consciousness was at work when, next, we launched the campaign to convince the AHFP (American Household Food Preparer, a new nonsexist politically correct term) that bacteria could not possibly grow in the extra-high acid content of Best All Mayonnaise. Bolognese & Bolognese represented both Kittridge's and Best All, so one hand slathered the other with money and salad dressing as we prepared a luncheon using mayonnaise in everything from drinks to dessert. Campaigns for gelatin deserts, instant rice, canned apples, powdered soup, whipped nondairy toppings kept the Kittridge's name in neon for all to see. The corporate food caravan rolled on as our head shots were stapled to press releases for ham butt, and in certain newspaper ads Gunnar and I could be found smiling enthusiastically at a very long salami.

Eleven

When we weren't on the road promoting ourselves or selling products at conventions, we were at Kittridge's. Friends gave up trying to see us. We missed christenings, bar mitzvahs and wakes. I even missed Wally's wedding to Fatima. A Saturday night in Brooklyn, it might as well have taken place in Egypt, so unlikely was my leaving Kittridge's on a busy weekend evening. We sent a gift of flowers. They sent photographs. They looked happy, sticking wedding baklava in each other's mouths. Fatima wore an exotic white caftan and flowers were tucked in around her veil. In the next shot she gazed up at her hero, as Wally looked straight at the camera, supremely, superbly victorious; he had found his happiness. Fatima was visibly pregnant. Pictures of the baby followed quickly, a dark, sturdy little thing who took after his mother.

Soon after the baby's birth, Wally and Fatima came to Kittridge's one afternoon to show us little Wally. They were oblivious to their surroundings and completely taken with their baby. Fatima breast-fed, slipped the baby back into his carriage, undid his diapers and cleaned his bottom while the Wall Street crowd downed cocktails and power lunches.

Fatima told me she had started working for her uncle as a

part-time pushcart vendor selling falafels on a busy corner of Montague Street. She missed her family, especially now that there was little Wally. "You are my only sister here," she announced. "That is why I must ask you to be the baby's godmother." She ceremoniously handed me Wally IV.

"Could be worse," said Gunnar later. "Just means getting presents at birthday, right?"

"It means if they drop dead, we get him," I explained. I was putting the finishing touches to my toenails with something called Red-Hot Red.

Gunnar weighed the idea. "With Wally is maybe still a possibility, but Fatima is survivor. She will be around for long time. What she is selling now?"

"Falafels." No one would see these nails now that the weather was turning colder, but occasional brush practice helped me keep my painting hand.

"We ate one once, right?"

I thought of the Middle Eastern dinner we had the first night we first met. I ate grape leaves from his fingers.

"Is served with some kind sauce—?"

"You ever think about getting married?" Nail brush posed in midair, toes wet and glowing fiery red, like ten little coals at the end of my feet. The words had tumbled out, unexpectedly, brought on, perhaps, by Wally and Fatima's visit.

Gunnar cleared his throat, walked to the windows, raised and lowered the blinds.

"I don't believe in marriage."

He poured himself a soda. Ralph nudged Gunnar's knees and watched as he drank. Might there be a little snack in his dog future? Sanguine Ralph, who took whatever came and was glad. Not once had he ever seen food come out of our refrigerator; still, he sat, ears perked, tail wagging, and hoped. Ralph the optimist.

"Marriage is shaky thing. What peoples think is keeping them together is also breaking them apart. Like eggshell, very delicate. Is not just love. Look, my parents. They had good thing, everything congenial, until my father wants for my mother to live with him in Russia. My father could not live in Finland, my mother would not come to Russia. My father could not change job, my mother would not learn Russian language. Never they live together in same place. So always I was thinking, If I love someone we gonna do all things together, work, live, then we will be together. Simple. Like us."

"We've definitely achieved the together part. Think it's time to move on to wedding rings?"

"Wait until we have big restaurant review." He was throwing me a bone. I wasn't jumping.

"Is wrong time to consider marriage. If we marry too soon, it will only break us apart, you will see."

Share enough Thanksgivings and Christmas Eves with strangers and you will come to see them as relatives. By default, waiters became the friends we no longer saw, our ipso facto family. Though I missed Ginger's birthday, Frenchie's homecoming and Rayburn's graduation, when Harmon was inducted into the Society of Tastevins, I managed to make the event, clapping like a proud relative. Skin of our skin, he was one of ours. Tears welled up in my eyes as four spindly-legged, pot-bellied Chevaliers de Tastevins dressed in ceremonial medieval garb crowned him and pinned a medallion on his chest.

The moment was pure Harmon Borsch. Had he been an olive, Harmon would have dripped oil on the floor right then and there. Unmitigated grease. I kissed his cheek, and my lips felt like I had just applied Chap Stick. Harmon beamed at me.

"Mom!" he said proudly.

It was late October, the city air seemed crisp and clean, even though you breathed in what the trucks breathed out. One of our waiters had just quit, and the rest of us rushed around the dining room nervously folding napkins, brushing last night's crumbs off chair cushions, removing gum balls with solvent, sweeping up cigarette butts from under tables. Harmon, wearing his Medal de Chevalier, was sweating as he hurriedly stocked the bar. When we finally sat down for a rushed family dinner before service, all the waiters were angry at Norman Didson for dumping us and leaving us so short-handed on a busy night.

"What can you expect? The man's entire career consisted of chili houses and burger joints," said MG. Norman had been a red-faced, stocky Irishman, overweight and out of breath at the table. His unruly red hair had never appeared combed. MG's family tree was rooted in staunch Mayflower stock.

"Strictly corned beef," Denby, our resident playwright, agreed.

"Norman once described a Pommard '82 as a 'dicey little number,'" MG said disgustedly.

Harmon was chewing bread thoughtfully, his cheeks full as a squirrel. "Actually, it *is* a dicey little number."

"Harmon," MG whined, "we went over the menu with Norm a million times. He *never* got it."

"Okay, okay, so he wasn't family," Harmon agreed reluctantly.

"Nor-mann? Forgait hees fehce!" agreed Andre. A sophisticated French Jew who had grown up in Algiers, he was the only one of us who had ever had servants. He spoke four languages and had come to America to visit, but never found the time or inclination to return home. He considered himself above the petty squabbles of the other waiters and was amused by the rest of us.

"For what reason you hire 'eem, 'Armon?"

Harmon rarely had to defend himself with this group who, under all other circumstances, basked in the light of his flattering soft pink lightbulb.

"He added a kind of chophouse je-ne-sais-quoi glow to the room, don't you think?"

"Perhaps we never made him comfortable enough here," Michael, our in-house minister, offered. MG was a snob and Michael was a Methodist. He had majored in theology and minored in political science, two topics he used to morally browbeat the rest of the waiters.

"Fa-ther Mi-chael, climbing into your pulpit again?" MG sang.

"I resent, I absolutely detest when you speak to me like that."

"Ees rilly not nahce, Emgee," cautioned Andre.

Denby had set the family table so that it was ready for the Queen of England, should she happen to drop in. Andre looked at the fully set table uncomprehendingly. "Denbee, why you do all zees work every night. A fork ees enough. Ees joost us, joost la famille."

I knew Norman would write us, telling us where to send his

last check, but the letter I received a week later was not the letter I had expected. I showed it to Gunnar, whose face fell when he read it.

" . . . You owe me back pay, some sixty hours for which I never received fair compensation over the months I worked at your establishment. In all the other places I have worked as a waiter I was paid an hourly rate except yours. According to the Labor Department, the kind of flat 'shift fee' you paid your waiters was and is illegal. I would appreciate you putting this matter right, as I need the money. A copy of this letter has been forwarded to the Labor Board and to each person on your current waiting staff. I hope they will join me in my current lawsuit against Kittridge's Restaurant."

Our accountants, Harry and Larry, were a father-and-son team. Harry, a seventy-year-old CPA, liked to whack his thirty-year-old son's head with a rolled-up newspaper whenever he made a mistake on the adding machine. The Gittners, two pear-shaped men, were the bruised fruit of the accounting profession.

"You pay your waiters a flat rate for the seven or eight hours they work instead of an hourly rate, right?" Harry reviewed the situation.

"Actually, is because *they* requested this method of payment."

"Sure, because they make more money that way. We worked it out on paper before we agreed to what they wanted, remember, Sport?" Harry reminded Gunnar. "You also agreed to turn their credit card tips into cash every evening. So *you* pay the taxes on that money, they *don't*, Sport."

"They go home every night with cash they don't pay taxes on. No wonder they're so happy," his son Larry agreed. "I should only work for you." Harry whacked him on the side of the head with a newspaper.

Somewhere in the recesses of my memory appeared the image of our first manager, Mert, a small man with a big head whom the waiters had nicknamed the Mole. The Mole had warned me about this. "All you need is one person, just one, to write a letter to the Labor Department about this method of payment, and you're in big trouble."

"No one would do that to us," I had argued.

"Is family," Gunnar admonished the Mole.

Larry sharpened pencils while Harry gave us his sage advice.

"Wait, you'll hear from the Labor Department. You'll get a lawyer. You'll proceed."

The letter from the Labor Department arrived two weeks later. Norman's complaint had opened the door to any and all waiters who had ever worked for us to join in his action and present a case against us for unlawfully withholding monies from them. Even though the money we'd paid over a period of almost two years added up to twice the amount the waiters would have received by being paid an hourly wage, legally the Labor Department wanted to see hourly wages on our books, and nothing else would do.

We consulted a law firm that specialized in negotiations with the Labor Department. The firm had three floors of specialists working in cubicles located off labyrinthine corridors connected by interdepartmental stairways and three banks of internal elevators.

"Cooperate and maybe the case will be confined to a smaller number of people," the labor lawyer who had been assigned to our case advised. The thin, earnest, sallow-faced man, who nervously folded and unfolded his hands on his desk, leaned towards us as he spoke. "The best you can hope for is to keep the case to your present staff of five rather than everyone who ever worked for you since you opened up almost two years ago. In this kind of case, people smell money. All loyalty goes out the door. They'll be after any buck they can get."

"They'd never do that to us," I sputtered.

Gunnar was no longer so sure.

"We make big mistake. Christ to hell, now we gonna pay. Is old story. We are on way up, so we gonna get kicked in ass by people who are closest. Of course they want piece of what we have. They keep business running while we are away. They feel they deserve piece of our success because they help to make it. First we are tasting cream, next we are sitting in shit."

A legal crisis provided an opportunity to build one of those islands of intimacy couples sometimes enjoy. The case was like a mud slide, and every time we appeared to fall deeper in, we grew closer. Gunnar held me at night with a fierce possession that reminded me of little Wally. He held me while we slept, and if I moved to turn to my other side, his grip tightened. Sometimes he woke with a start. "Don't go," he panicked, like a sleepwalker aroused and frightened.

The clinical sexual requests had stopped. Romance was on a roll. Instead of coaxing our bodies into new positions, there were gentler touches, body strokes that were the difference between lovemaking and fucking. The more we worried, the more we clung to each other. Were the waiters for us or against us? We lived all day just to get ourselves to the bedroom at night, and once there, sex made everything else fuzzy. We were love-drunk. Heat rose from our bodies like vapors off a swamp.

We made love and forgot to use a condom, *protection*, as Lilly once called it.

The more anxious the case made Gunnar, the more he wanted to know he was pleasing me. He hardly needed to prove himself sexually, yet he had become insistent about satisfying me. He would ask repeatedly during and after sex if I had liked something he had done. Do you like it? Tell me you like it. Do you want more? Tell me how good it feels. Tell me you need it. How much? He was having a crisis of confidence, and he wanted to be *told* things: how hot he made me feel, how wet, how full. His sexual compulsion was to please, and I luxuriated in his attentions to my body. I discovered, however, that being the lucky recipient of his favors was a heavy responsibility. I had to think of new ways to please myself in order to please him. Gunnar's experimentation had left few things untried besides the forbidden fruit of conceiving a baby. And so it happened one night, as it always does and as it always will, that at a moment of high-pitched pleasure, I bit his neck and asked him to enter me, *now*. It was a karmic mishap. A cosmic crisscross.

His poor business judgment had thrown him as hard and heavy as a sumo wrestler might, but not nearly as hard and far as his next mistake. Wearing nothing but his skin, a poor innocent in the house of love, Gunnar entered me while I hummed away like a queen bee.

"*Come*," I buzzed while he groaned, "Come in me."

I couldn't help it. Call it a test; I wanted us to come together. I was getting closer, so close, so sure, so confident of that sensation, so certain of the pleasure of pulsing, of having him while he had me. But *having him*, that's what mattered most.

"*Come inside me, now.*"

And he did.

At first, as he lay on me, he seemed particularly proud. "Was good?" Then he rolled off my body and came to slowly, as though waking from a dream. He had never risked impregnating me. He had gotten too caught up with pleasing me. Within minutes of returning to his senses, he was horrified by how far astray his genitals had just led him.

"Guess I'm just a devil woman," I yawned.

"Don't make joke," he fumed.

"Well." I was beginning to get a little concerned by his reaction. "It was the heat of the moment, I guess."

"Jesu, is not one moment, is our life. *Is rest of our life.*" He leaned over the bed and, in a dramatic gesture worthy of Dana Andrews, ran his fingers through his hair. "What have we done? This is worst time in world to risk making a baby."

He was finally coming around. *A* baby. The man was starting to use articles.

It had come to this. I sat on the bathtub rim, dropped the little pill into my urine, and stared at the test tube I was holding. The moment was pure chemistry. I thought of all the blue things: hold your breath till your face turns blue, wait till the moon turns blue. . . . So out of keeping was pregnancy to my entire generation that these days a woman had to piss blue before she knew she was pregnant.

He asked me every day, "You are getting period yet? No? Nothing? You are sure?"

"You've done everything but look in my underwear, will you cut it out? It's too early yet."

I had never seen a more worried Gunnar. He had night

sweats, woke up in the middle of the night, went down into the kitchen and ate chocolate cake. He drank too much. He brought several beers upstairs with him at night. The way he was eating, I'd have thought he was pregnant.

"I am not ready to be father," he choked between bites. "I need more time."

"For what?"

"To practice."

"On what, cabbage heads?"

Gunnar had begun to bring food up into the apartment every night after service. I watched him stuff it in. A big favorite of his was herring and buttermilk.

"How can you eat that?"

"You would like some?"

"Pickled fish and milk? Didn't your mother teach you how to eat?"

"I told you. My mother is worst cook in universe. Grandmother was good cook. Big vodka drinker, but good cook."

"Your father's mother?"

"No, no, mother's mother. Finns are vodka drinkers, none of that Aquavit piss for us. From Russian domination," he explained, taking another swig of buttermilk.

"I don't think I can watch you drink that."

"Piima," he belched, "Viili, sour milk. Good stuff. Brings memories." We had no table, so we ate on the bed. He adjusted the pillows behind his neck and popped another herring.

"When my father came, he and my mother would sit in my grandmother's bathhouse, sauna, all of us," he said, smiling. "My grandmother would be hanging the sausages there to dry over hot coals, saunamakkara, poromakkara, smoked reindeer tongue. My father was drinking beer, everybody sweating. Was like living room, everyone together."

He put down the food which he had been enjoying.

"I cried every time my father left."

"And when you left your mother?"

"We had fight. I blamed her for what happened with my father. Then I come to America. I think, If I go, she will follow me, and they will be together again. It was stupid idea of young person," he said caustically. "They were good pair. Never fighting. Just always they were apart. Never together in what they did. He spoke her language, she couldn't speak his, he wanted to travel, she stayed home, he read Turgenev, she read beauty magazine, he loved her, she loved." He paused. "She loved *me*." He was no longer speaking but thinking, and when he came out of his trance he spoke as though he assumed I had been following his train of thought.

" . . . And then I left—"

He called his mother once a month. He never told me what they said, and of course they spoke in Finnish so I was at a disadvantage as far as uncovering family secrets.

"How is she?" I would ask.

"The same," he would answer.

"What does that mean?" I would press.

"She misses me."

"Why don't you send for her?"

"She won't come."

"Why don't you go to her?"

"I have you to love, right here."

"I'll go with you. We could take a vacation."

"Inari is long way away, and Rovaniemi is ugly."

It must have been frightening to leave a piece of yourself behind in a place that was so emotionally far away that you could never go back to reclaim it.

"They let you bring memories back through customs these days, you know. They don't even open up the baggage and check."

"Very funny. Sure you don't want to drink Piima?"

During the next two months, while waiting for our case to be heard and waiting to see if I was pregnant, Gunnar told family stories that were filled with elks, Laapi aunts, homemade liquor, cold lake-water swims, blue-eyed, flaxen-haired cousins and boiled wool clothing.

I had no such exotic stories, not even ordinary ones. If I had cousins, I didn't even know them. I had no living grandparents; there was no extended family, no cousins, aunts, uncles. There were distant relatives, an aunt I had met once, but I didn't remember her. I could not remember family events, not because my parents didn't know how to make and keep dates; they were wizards at business appointments. They simply had no use for family. But the want of it had made it seem all the more interesting to me and worth having. Both my parents had been only children and so was I.

"That's how it is," Lilly had explained when I was a child. "You grow up, and there's no one else. Get used to it. It has its advantages."

"Of course, I've tried to explain your position." Harmon sipped his brandy and took a long, thoughtful puff on his cigar. "I've tried to get them to see things your way."

"See things our way? They've already been paid." I was exasperated.

"Yes, but the law says the opportunity is still there, if you see what I mean."

He shifted around uncomfortably in his seat. A case of moral ants in his pants, I thought.

"You know how it is. They all have such *needs*."

Harmon explained that Andre wanted to return to Algiers, Denby wanted time to complete his play, MG planned on sailing someplace warm where he would never have to do laundry, and Michael wanted to fight the good fight.

"How much money do they think there is in this case?" I asked indignantly.

"How much money is the business worth?" Harmon flashed a Burt Lancaster smile.

That night Gunnar and I sat up in bed, both unable to fall asleep. We turned on the light and thought out loud.

"They all have reasons for joining Norman in the suit against us," I said.

"And Harmon is knowing every reason they are having," said Gunnar with a deep, distrustful sigh as he turned off the light.

Every day a man from the Labor Department showed up to review our books. He wore the drip-dry uniform of the civil servant. Over his polyester he wore a hand-knitted maroon vest. He accepted several cups of coffee but refused the sweeter bribes of chocolate cake or ice cream sundaes. He filled out pink and green forms in triplicate while his pocket calculator burped sinister rhythms.

Meanwhile, we tried to negotiate a settlement in order to avoid a full-blown case. We explained our position to MG who shifted uncomfortably in his chair. Where once there was familiarity and ease, now there was stiffness and embarrassment.

Usually, MG had the grace of a sports car, backing up, revving forward, sliding in and out of tight spaces. Outwardly he was smooth and unruffled, but inwardly he was a complicated engine, ailing and cranky most of the time. Tall, lanky, in his late twenties, genteel and polite, he had the confidence of the well-read and well-schooled, though otherwise the silver spoon hung heavy in his mouth.

Our efforts to use MG as an intermediary failed. He sideswiped problematic turns as though life were a landscape fraught with possible disaster and he, a speedster in the Indianapolis 500.

"Well, I'll *try* telling them, but I can't promise. We're meeting at Harmon's tonight."

"Harmon's?"

"We've been meeting there every day, with our lawyer, Harmon's cousin Stanley."

I shot a look at Gunnar. I had been cooking. I was hot, my hair disheveled, I smelled of turnips and smoke. Gunnar held the reservation book close against his chest as though his heart would fall out.

"We've really come together as a group. We're cohesive, talking and listening to each other. Can you imagine? *Us*, listening to each other? You'd be proud. We've decided it's all or nothing, one for all and all for one, real Musketeer-like. We're going to talk it out until we all agree to do the same thing, either all stay out or all jump in."

"Sounds like a great pool date," I said.

"And the credit goes to you for making such a warm family atmosphere with no hard feelings and all."

The next day, we again cornered MG before service.

"How did the meeting go? Did they vote yet?"

"I'm sorry, I can't tell you anything."

"We just want to know if the staff would be willing to negotiate a settlement—"

"I understand, but the process takes time. Speak to Michael. He's in charge now."

"We thought Harmon was spearheading the drive."

"I wish. Harmon's too busy right now with his sommelier thing. Color photo in the *Wine Spectator* in two weeks. So now it's Michael, complete with Robert's Rules of Order. Liberal fascist Nazi," he added in disgust. "Let's face it, you're in trouble with Minderman at the helm."

Michael had a pious shell that could not be cracked. At his job interview at Kittridge's, he had sat so stiff and upright, his back never touching the chair, like God's little arrow, I thought. A handsome male body whose perfect proportions got stuck with a mean spirit, like a star caught on the branches of an old dead tree.

"You are sure you want this job?" Gunnar had asked him doubtfully. Michael had several degrees and was ordained in the Methodist Church.

"My life is service," Michael explained earnestly, petting Ralph's ears as the dog licked the shine off Michael's black wing-tipped shoes.

Unable to get any satisfaction from MG, and knowing we would never get any from Michael, we turned once again to Harmon. We had heard that some of our waiters were now considering joining Norman in the suit.

"Can't say," said Harmon.

Harmon's rubbery face winced, his shoulders hunched up

like an innocent. His mouth opened, speechless, a dry fountain unable to spurt. He held up his empty palms in a final gesture of powerlessness. Harmon couldn't help himself. He wasn't a liar exactly, he just wasn't very interested in the truth. Wiggling out from under, he explained.

"Can I help it if they look to me for help? They needed someone, and Stan is cheap."

"Maybe *you* could explain the unfairness of getting us on a legal technicality. Remind them that we've always been fair to them."

"Why me?" he asked innocently. "Michael's the one in charge."

"Because they trust you. Michael worships you."

Michael was Harmon's groupie, a six-foot WASP practicing a Jewish accent. He loved repeating Harmon's jokes, even though we'd heard them all before.

"I'm getting to be a real mee-shoo-geena, wouldn't you say?"

But Michael was too adoring even for Harmon's taste.

"My echo chamber," Harmon would complain. "Please, Michael, go to joke school. You're ruining my best material."

"We don't want to talk to Michael," I whined, pleading with Harmon to reconsider. "You know how caught up he gets, how stiff he is."

"Michael'll be all right as soon as he gets laid," Harmon predicted thoughtfully.

"We don't have time to wait," said Gunnar.

Two weeks later, our lawyer called to tell us it was too late for negotiations. Since the Labor Department had invested one of their employees' time for over two weeks, it couldn't drop the case without showing a profit. The Labor Department had also decided to limit the suit to our present, working staff, excluding Norman Didson who was no longer on our payroll. A date for our hearing had been set.

Working with the waiters became stressful for Gunnar and me. We got on each other's nerves and were disappointed in each other. The secrets that had made us human and acceptable to each other had turned us into aliens. We worked alongside each other diligently, relying on professionalism to pull us through, like cars on automatic. We hardly spoke to each other and confined our conversations to polishing silver and reordering wine glasses.

On the morning of the hearing, Gunnar and I met our lawyer for coffee and donuts in the basement cafeteria of the World Trade Center where the Labor Department offices were located. The cafeteria, over two blocks long, wore the official blue and orange of New York. Justice reigned supreme as civil employees of every shape and color enjoyed their fifteen-minute breaks while the newest wave of legal immigrants cleared the tables and swept the floor.

The Labor Department offices had none of the pizazz of the old City Hall buildings, no stone carvings, no wedding-cake moldings. This was not the architecture of democracy, just the poorly maintained hallways of a megalithic new building already in disrepair, housing miles of red tape. Nor were the offices of the Labor Department bristling with activity. Women workers padded around in soft bedroom slippers, and men carried thermos bottles to and from their desk, filling and refilling from a water tank down the hall. The place had the spiritual atmosphere of a nursing home, and the civil employees seemed to be licking their wounds and getting well slowly. In contrast to the interiors, the views out the windows were breathtaking. We stood in this diocese of power, papal seat of greed and political machinations, admiring the long gray stretches of city from forty floors up.

We were led to a windowless conference room and seated around a sturdy green table, the type found in high school principals' offices. The waiters were already there, and we walked in on Harmon telling a short, ribald joke.

"We'll all feel better once this is behind us," Harmon assured us, as though the hearing was just business penicillin.

MG bit his nails, uncomfortable and sullied by his contact with the world of the underdog. Denby, wearing sunglasses, seemed uneasy, mystified as to how he had gotten there. Andre took long, bored sucks on a tortoise cigarette holder. Only Michael seemed comfortable and happy in these surroundings. He was busy arranging a pile of notes and laughed at Harmon's jokes as he handed index cards to the others.

The supervisor in charge of the case stood up and introduced himself. Mr. Howie was a jittery but agreeable man with the deeply lined face and gray pallor of a chain smoker. Harmon, who did not smoke, produced a silver cigarette lighter and rose each time the supervisor brought forth a new cigarette.

"So now, let the bargaining begin," smiled Mr. Howie with the cordiality of an emcee.

He suggested the waiters make the first bid as to a specific money settlement and led them into an adjoining room where they could privately decide on a figure.

Ten minutes later Mr. Howie emerged, alone.

"Greedy," Mr. Howie explained knowingly. "They had their hearts set on the whole enchilada."

We sat tight while Mr. Howie finished his next cigarette and he told us about his favorite restaurants. His favorite dish was sausage and peppers at a little place on Mott Street.

He returned to the other room, and we sat by ourselves for another ten minutes, after which he emerged.

"It always comes down to vacation plans, spending habits. The more specific their plans, the harder it is for them to compromise," he explained.

He shared a long list of more cheap-eats restaurants including a place on Broome. "Only open when the red light is on," he winked.

"Whorehouse cuisine," I said to Gunnar after Mr. Howie put out his cigarette and nervously ducked back into the waiters' room. "What will they think of next?"

He emerged ten minutes later, apologetic, more nervous than before, and now openly annoyed.

"That's some crew you've got in there," he said. "They can't agree on anything." Another cigarette, another restaurant report, this one a little strained in its cheerfulness. We listened with limited interest as he described black paella with squid ink from a great little Cuban-Chinese place on Queens Boulevard.

Mr. Howie started traveling between rooms like a frequent flyer. "They want the full amount paid in two months." He sighed as he sat. "They don't get it yet."

Finally we made the first offer. Fifty percent of the total amount owed to be paid over two years in eight equal payments.

Mr. Howie shuttled between the conference rooms six more times as a Labor Department diplomat, carrying with him his invisible attaché of professional negotiating techniques.

"Very different types, those boys. Sensitive, but ornery. How did you all ever get along before all this happened?"

"Was one big happy family," Gunnar said automatically.

"Oh, shut up with that already," I snapped.

By his eighth try, Mr. Howie was looking more and more like Hugh Downs as the case began to resemble "Let's Make a Deal" and "Family Feud" rolled into one.

We finally settled on fifty percent to be paid over one year in four installments.

"Can we fire them?" I asked Mr. Howie.

"Not cool," he answered, taking a long, thoughtful drag on his last cigarette. "Not cool, at least not right away."

Soon, Gunnar would install a time clock, taxes would be taken out of paychecks, salaries fully declared, no tips would be converted into cash at the end of each evening. W-2's and W-10's were handed out. In a moral victory for our side, Mr. Howie assured us that the Internal Revenue Service would challenge the waiters' income tax statements for four previous years. Apparently, if you messed with one government agency, you messed with them all.

I looked out the window. From the fortieth floor of the World Trade Center, I watched the first snow of the year covering the top of the city's spiky silhouette in feathery strokes. The snow had come, and with it my period. Late, but as vivid and red as my newly painted toenails. The business was forming around us, falling into place like the snow. Or, maybe, like the abominable snowman.

Twelve

The cold, dry, winter air was more crisp than bitter. Sunlight cheered and warmed Kittridge's dining room. Even the most demanding lunch customer seemed friendly and easy to serve on a day as promising as this. I stood behind the bar in my whites, taking a break from the kitchen. I was sipping coffee when an aging Howdy Doody walked in. His faded red hair was slicked down behind his ears and swept high off his forehead. He had freckles and big blue eyes magnified by his glasses. He looked like he had been dressed by a Hong Kong tailor, his suit finely crafted but the fabric strangely foreign. The small white polka dots that danced across his blue worsted suit were set off by a red-and-white-striped tie. The man was a walking barber pole.

He handed the waiter his raincoat but held onto his hat. I heard him request a large table where there was room to place his Stetson. What kind of man invites his hat to eat with him? As he followed the waiter to his table, he passed by the bar, flashed me a politician's grin and handed me a two-inch alligator molded out of gummy green rubber. It would bring me good luck, he said. As I turned it over in my hands he added, proudly, "I own the copyright on that. But I'll tell you all about myself when we meet together for lunch."

Which sounded like something I didn't want to do.

His card read *Albert Becker, Toy Manufacturer.* Every time he came, he brought with him another rubber doll. Porcupines in high heels, gorillas playing guitars, hound dogs in baseball caps, chickens wearing toques. We were treated to the entire line of gummy creatures which soon found their way throughout the restaurant, moving into the empty spaces in drawers and shelves around the restaurant like little uninvited guests. There are certain businessmen who, after a lifetime of eating out, become restaurant watchers, curious about how they are run, fascinated by the mystery behind the kitchen door. Mr. Becker, or Mr. B as he liked to be called, was such a man.

When Gunnar emerged from his office, wearing his best suit, he cocked his head in the direction of Mr. B, who sat alone at the table reading the menu and sipping his drink.

"Mr. Becker. Very important man. Wants piece of business."

"What business?"

"Ours," he said and, with a knowing look, took off to join the man and his hat for lunch before I could respond.

I'd known Gunnar was up to something more expansive than hiring a public relations firm. He'd closeted himself in his office, spending hours on the phone, entertaining a steady stream of new faces day and night, hard-core business types in super-slick threads. I knew he was dealing himself a new hand. Blackjack. When I asked him about the calls from names I didn't recognize, Gunnar would only say they were important.

I paid little attention. I was busy planning a spring menu, trying to decide whether I was disappointed or relieved that I wasn't having a baby. I led a complicated life. I was having a complicated reaction to the pregnancy scare and the law case. I assumed Gunnar was too. We'd both thrown ourselves into work, and so when I'd noticed his madman-moving-mountains look, I wasn't surprised. I was all too familiar with Gunnar's Dale-Carnegie-of-the-streets mode. It had turned our home into a business, brought us over the Brooklyn Bridge, and found us Henkelbottle's. So when he alluded to his secret deal, I just waited. Sooner or later, he'd have to tell me. He would need my signature.

"Wants to be backer. Wants to buy business. Is our chance to move, get big."

"Bigger is not better," I warned. I'd known for some time that Gunnar was hoping to find an angel to take him uptown. But looking for a backer was a lot like looking into a refrigerator that never had what you wanted to eat. Gunnar's hungry ambition craved steak, but all he had found was celery. Celery is not an exciting vegetable by itself, but it is always happy to be included in a soup that stars, say, potato. Were we Mr. B's potato? Was he our celery?

Gunnar was checking his tie in the mirror behind the bar.

"Just I am asking for you to have lunch with us. Listen to guy."

"But I don't want to go to lunch with him. I'm not sure I trust him."

"He wants to meet you." Gunnar could believe in anything or anyone as long as it served his purpose.

"I don't want to move. I don't want to get any bigger than we are."

"Just first meet this guy. Anyway, you got to keep eye on what I am doing." He kissed me as he marched out to the dining room. "And please," he said, "be nice."

Mr. B was, I discovered, a consummate salesman adept at selling himself. In return for the compliments he gave out generously, he expected the best table in the house and our undivided attention while he told story after story. According to the waiters, he was a poor tipper, but he was so gregarious and congenial that the waiters liked him despite his ten-percent gratuities. By the end of lunch, I supposed I would have bought a used car from him, though the only product he was selling was himself. He was by nature and temperament a most persistent suitor.

The luncheon had started out with conciliatory questions. He asked after our health. Were we getting enough rest? Eating well? Did we have an exercise program? Take enough time off to relax? Assuring us that health was everything, he launched into giving advice. He was concerned about some of our higher-priced specials. Would we consider adding into the bread basket a few slices of Erwasher's pumpernickel with raisins? Did we find making our own ice cream cost-effective? He wanted to know the number of chairs and tables, and he had a few thoughts about our color scheme. He hoped we wouldn't mind these suggestions, it was necessary to understand his point of view, his perspective, he must feel comfortable sharing his thoughts with us. Had we ever considered Kittridge's-to-go? Would we consider a line of frozen take-out dinners? Did we think there was a growing market for green teas? Medicinal broths? A chocolate bialy?

Lunch flew by, and with it a bevy of concepts. He had so many ideas, so many *wonderful* ideas for us. There wasn't time to waste. But first he wanted to get to know us. "In business there can be no strangers. Going into business with someone is like falling in love." Who was I to argue that business was not like love with its seductions and betrayals? So began our courtship with Mr. B.

"This guy moves fast," said Gunnar as he filled in his calendar with Albert Becker dates. In a week, the three of us would meet for lunch at the hottest new restaurant uptown. Uptown, where Kittridge's ought to be, Becker had added. "What do you think it means?" Gunnar asked.

"Maybe he wants to marry us."

What followed were a series of Albert Becker phone calls. The calls were quintessential Mr. B, full of business savvy and enthusiastic play, perfectly aligned, like an eclipse. A day had not gone by when he didn't think of us. He had been up all night, thinking. Were we interested in putting brown rice on our menu? Or a simple vegetarian plate? A low-cal special also seemed timely. Had we been to Bloomingdale's to taste their new frozen yogurt? How did we feel about opening up next to the United Nations? Could we run a steak joint? How did we feel about franchising?

In one week we received ten phone calls; in each call a new idea was born. Mr. B's ideas were like his children. None were bad, all were good, and though there were too many of them, they all deserved to live. His ideas ranged from those close to home to more exotic ones, cooked up in that hothouse mind of his. Had we considered expanding next door into what was currently a dentist's office? He could imagine moving our kitchen downstairs, our toilets into the coatroom, the coatroom to the fireplace, and at the entrance a glass house, a mini arboretum. Or how did we feel about East Hampton? Branching out in Tokyo and Paris? I had to admit Mr. B added a certain zing to our days. On the other hand, I was struck by his intellectual changeability. Like some overactive gland, his brain threw off new and dangerous notions all the time.

On the day of our next luncheon, he called again.

"I am so looking forward to our luncheon date," he said sprightly, "that I am shining my shoes in anticipation." Did that mean I had to shine mine? I wore suede pumps just to be on the safe side.

He hadn't wanted us to think he was a "creature tied to the past," so he had picked the hottest uptown spot he knew. The walls were paneled in olive wood, the purple velvet banquettes felt like butter, and you could almost see your reflection in the satin moire drapes. As the harried maitre d' checked our names in his reservation book our host flashed his biggest campaign grin and handed Jean-Luc a mini pair of wind-up sneakers that walked across his podium. Jean-Luc diplomatically caught the toy shoes as they were about to fall off and offered to return them. No, no, Mr. B patted him on the shoulder, they would bring him good luck.

As we slid into our banquette, I considered the possible consequences of going into business with someone who had a chronic case of the terrible twos. Dishes would be garnished with gummy little creatures, waiters sporting baseball mitts would serve tables made from Lego sets, while battery-operated model cars would buzz and whir across the dining room floors as astonished customers bent down mid-bite to see what had just rolled under the table, over their feet.

Mr. B believed in the power of illustrations, so he had brought with him a few pictures. He opened a folder as we sipped our cocktails. The first was a yellowing picture of his dead wife, when she was young, playing tennis, a thin brunette caught by the camera mid-jump as she arched to whack a ball with her racquet. He had only dated blondes before her, he explained, more beautiful than she, but his wife had been so vivacious, and had played tennis so well, that she had won him over; he had given up his freedom. He spoke of himself in old-fashioned bachelor terms, as though he had been a prize she had won. His emotional life seemed set in amber, atrophied by the loss of the one person he had so long ago allowed himself to love. He talked on about his brief but happy marriage, his devotion to his two college-age sons. Yet it was his bachelorhood that seemed to be the salient fact of his life.

A second picture kept us company during appetizers, introducing The Richest Man in Mexico. He sat like a heavy dumpling, very old and turtle-like on his terracotta palazzo surrounded by green ferns and tropical flowers. In the next photo, The Heir to a Refrigerator Fortune waved to us from the snowy slopes of Switzerland.

The pictures were a trick he had used in the Far East when dealing with businessmen who did not speak his language. Everyone, he had discovered, understands a picture. And so he introduced his sons to us, in bathing suits and drinking sodas by a pool, thereby proving himself to be a man of substance and responsibility, as well as a man with wealthy and influential friends around the world. If our first course of photos had demonstrated Mr. B's character, our second course illustrated the broad nature of his humanitarian interests and his uncanny feel for trends. A newsclip photo showed a woman reclining on a hospital cot, her legs in inflated, balloon-like boots. The caption read "New Invention Helps Stimulate Circulation." According to Mr. B, this was an idea whose time had come, and he was one of the boots' prime investors.

He explained over our entree that for many years he had studied the Oriental science of faces with the well-known Professor Zhong. Mr. B had become a shrewd and accurate judge of character as it was revealed through the human face. Out came an obituary for a dead man who had pioneered termite control in America. Immediately after seeing this obituary, Mr. B had called the editor of the *Times* to say that there had been a mistake; the face in that picture could not possibly belong to a man who had anything to do with insects. Mr. B had been triumphant when the *Times* obit editor apologetically explained that, in fact, there had been a mistake and that the photograph in question belonged to a man who had pioneered in the field of music education.

One vodka martini and a bottle of wine later, we dug into dessert. For our final exhibit, we were shown a letter written to Mr. B by the president of Chock Full O' Nuts, a response to a letter sent by Mr. B suggesting that Chock add scones to their menu. The president cursorily thanked Mr. B for his idea. He appreciated Mr. B's sending the samples but did not think scones were Chock's sort of thing. Only two years later, Mr. B said ominously, with a sad shake of his head as he refolded the letter and stuck it back in his manila folder, the great Chock went under. He shrugged, pitying Chock. We all pitied Chock. If only the president had listened to Mr. B about love, life, and baked goods.

The profile he had painted of himself emerged. A man interested in things culinary, with an eye for trends. A family man with a sense of responsibility to those he took under his wing. A world traveler with wealthy friends. A great judge of character. Behind this solicitous picture, a shadowy profile emerged: a tasteless man fond of drawing attention to himself, a man not used to compromise, with an oblique sense of the Important Things in life. The moral to Mr. B's life's story seemed to hover between the phenomenological worlds of Ripley and Kafka.

Over cognacs he announced his plans. He was willing to buy thirty percent of our stock and finance a move uptown as soon as the right location was found. Uptown: Gunnar's dream zip code, a culinary landscape known for its cushioned chairs, padded walls, carpeted floors, tuxedoed maitre d's and cloth towels in the ladies' rooms. Finally, an offer. Mr. B could relax the thinking gears and turn off that mental light bulb. Finally he had proposed a deal. At the end of the evening Mr. B left a poor tip. On the way out I slipped the waiter a fifty-dollar bill.

It had become obvious that Mr. B made his calls from his favorite haunts: hotel lobbies, his pool's locker room, steam room, barbershop, his tennis club. The whistles from the lifeguard, the splashing sounds as bodies dove into water, made me wonder if I was receiving calls from a child away at a camp that specialized in, say, business sports. On one such aquatic phone call he suggested that in exchange for his advice, Gunnar and I give up another twenty percent of our stock so that in the end we would be fifty-percent partners. His expertise alone would earn us all the extra profits needed to generate the monies for a move uptown. I had my doubts. So far we had two luncheon dates and fifty phone calls. Every time we thought we had a deal, Mr. B had another creative business idea. We developed not one deal but many.

We received breathless and excited phone calls. He had been

jogging around the reservoir and stopped long enough to call us to set up an another appointment. He ran in place as he spoke. By any chance were we joggers? We could have our next meeting running together around the reservoir.

We did not jog, but even if we did, we had already invited our lawyer to our next meeting and we did not think he would come to a reservoir. Our lawyer Max did not believe in jogging. He was not a man who kept himself pretty. Mr. B panted and huffed, "Time is of the essence. If not now, when?" Gunnar thought the negotiation was at a sensitive point and that a deal was imminent. I waited and watched.

Paunchy, bald, brilliant Max was a putter-together of people and deals. He was not exactly the man to call when you were in small claims court. Max was not helpful in matters of petty injustice; he had seen too much of it. Very little in life surprised him. We had asked him to help us clinch the deal, or at least to help us find it, catch it and make it settle down.

When we met at Kittridge's for lunch, the table was set for five, as Mr. B had requested. The four of us sat down, Max, Mr. B, Gunnar and myself. And of course, the Stetson on its own chair. Max watched all this like a cat brought in to catch a rat. The afternoon got off on the wrong foot. Lunch at Kittridge's was crowded, our food was late and, according to Mr. B, cold. As we began to remind Mr. B of the things he'd offered, he accused us of naïveté. A kiss-and-punch routine began. We brought up his ideas and he accused us of misunderstanding. So help me God, *I* never said that. So help me God, *you* never said that. Like a refrain to a love song. His changes of mind were not due to greed, or even self-protection; they were part of his creativity. He had so many wonderful ideas, he reminded us. "I can't even count, that's how many I have." Any change of heart, any shift was due to his passionate faith in our business potential.

Our meeting no longer had the polite quality of a first date. Mr. B no longer asked us who we were and what we liked, but how much of his money we wanted to use and for what. In one more turnaround, he now offered half the monies he had earlier offered and suggested that we commit the rest. When Max reminded him that Gunnar and I were in no position to contribute personal monies, Mr. B's tactic was to treat us like a business gone wrong. In his scenario, Mr. B, through the power of clean and positive thinking, would lift us out of the gutter of our own mistakes into the realm of greater and greater profitability.

"Half of nothing is nothing," he reminded us, "and I am no Daddy Warbucks."

An incredulous Max jolted out of his reverie, lurched forward in his seat, and accidentally knocked Mr. B's hat to the floor. Mr. B jumped to his feet, accusing Max of carelessness, and as they both bent to retrieve the Stetson, Mr. B warned Max *not to touch his hat.*

When everyone had regained their composure, Mr. B smoothed his hat and again assured us all that his creative approach to business would prove to be more valuable than money. After all, wasn't that what we wanted? Not just the money, but the man? What were we to him, I wondered, but a businessman's version of Pygmalion?

Max looked at me, horrified, when Gunnar told Mr. B that his point was well taken. Gunnar's reluctance to stop nursing at the tit of this deal bothered me. Still, Gunnar could do nothing without me, and if all we'd lost was a talker, then we hadn't lost much. Over Max's objections, Gunnar persisted and agreed to meet with Mr. B one more time. At first I refused to go with him, but on Max's advice I accompanied him so that I could keep track of the deal's unravelings. Like a compulsive knitter, Mr. B pulled out hours of good work just to repeat one stitch. Never trust a man who hands out rubber dolls.

Our last meeting with Mr. B took place at Mr. B's tennis club, situated in a penthouse suite adjoining a swimming pool and rooftop garden on Sutton Place. We were met in the lobby of a forty-floor apartment building by a doorman who handed us over to a second doorman who handed us over to a muscular attendant in white tennis shorts who took us down a long corridor, up a flight of stairs, and put us on an elevator which opened up on the rooftop tennis courts. We were shown into the lounge area, a sunny room decorated in yellow and white, surrounded by glass doors that led to the enclosed wraparound terrace. Inside this club, it was perpetual summer with Astroturf floors throughout, wrought-iron patio furniture, padded chaises and glass-topped tables.

We arrived fifteen minutes early only to find Mr. B on his portable phone and the public phone, both. He had his back to us and hadn't seen us walk in. Though he was in his tennis shorts, he wore his hat pushed back on his head like an Alan Ladd tough guy. He looked and sounded like a man used to holding three phones at once, each with a different deal dangling on the other end. He was talking hundreds of thousands of dollars to someone else. It was like finding your lover in bed with a stranger. When I coughed, he spun around, got off the phone quickly, and apologized, saying that he hoped we had not gotten the wrong idea.

Mr. B insisted on walking us all around the club, which smelled of chlorine. We walked into the glass-enclosed terrace, stood on the Astroturf, and surveyed his world. The club looked out onto the East River and had an unobstructed view of the United Nations. He hated the handsome black building that loomed next door. It cast a shadow on the very spot where, when she was alive, his wife used to sit and read.

Clouds rolled across the big patch of open sky, birds twittered, yellow and green Day-Glo tennis balls sallied back and forth over the net. He wrinkled his nose and took a long deep breath like a sommelier. He could smell success, he said. His ability to whiff the rightness of people and situations was instinctual, he said. He looked at us and his nose continued to twitch. I expected him to start buzzing like a Geiger counter.

He took our hands, regretfully, like a long-lost lover. "It would be so nice to have a lovely couple like you all to myself." But, with the market the way it was, he had to limit his exposure while covering all the bases. This was the special brand of double-talk I had come to expect from him. He had decided, sadly, this deal was not for him alone. How did we feel about a consortium of backers? He could put one together. He knew a man, a fashion designer . . . we could get a loan . . . take the money . . . interest would be charged . . . profits and returns . . . 50–50 . . . 40–60 . . . he had learned . . . stock market . . . limit his exposure . . . cover all the bases. . . . His words fell like wet snow; nothing stuck. His plans could change in a day, an hour. All I could hear was his loneliness. Anyone smelling success and backing out at the same time was talking about life, not business.

Say, did we play tennis? Did we care to stick around and watch a few minutes of his game? He had discovered the truth in that old maxim, if you want to see how a man does business, watch him on the tennis court. But no, we couldn't. We had to get back, we had a restaurant to run. He walked us onto the elevator and took us through the tortuous maze of corridors. He assured us he would put together a group of investors. He took our hands and said again, "It would have been so very nice to have had you all to myself."

The doorman whistled up a cab for us. I shivered in my coat. The sun had dropped, and it was winter again.

"One moment he gives me the creeps, the next I feel sorry for him," I complained to Gunnar during the cab ride home. Save my breath, I thought. Feel sorry for myself, I thought. My boyfriend has fallen head over heels with something I don't want.

"But how about this consortium idea? Franchise is good idea too." I could hear his wheels turning. A deal is a deal is a deal.

"I won't go along with it."

"You gonna love it. We gonna get rich, then we get married. Big wedding bells is ringing."

"I can't hear a thing," I said.

Soon after, his head filled with ideas put there by Mr. B, Gunnar actively courted other potential backers. A married couple deep into coin-operated laundromats and a leathery-faced Greek luncheonette magnate named Steve Krokadopolis. Each new potential deal seemed more complicated than the next. Numbers went flying, percentages following like tails behind kites on a windy day. Forty thousand, sixty thousand, one hundred thousand. Liquid assets, fixed assets, long-term liabilities. Move, stay put, downward curves, upward trends. The ins and outs of Gunnar's deals became harder and harder to follow, though I understood enough of the basics.

"Greek guy is offering car, apartment, big salary."

This had nothing to do with food; we could have been selling anything. It wasn't because we were good. It was because we were willing.

"Laundry people is making all-cash offer."

It was the business of business.

"Do you see how good is gonna be for us?" His enthusiasm, almost contagious.

But all I could see was Mr. B wrinkling his nose, breathing in that sweet smell of success, holding our hands and wishing he had us all to himself.

Thirteen

Gunnar groped for the phone. It was 3:00 A.M. The caller had woken us both. Gunnar sounded concerned, but he looked exasperated.

"Okay, okay. I will be right over. Put some ice—Don't do nothing till I get there."

I was still groggy as he put on his pants and explained.

"Dolores has had big fight with John. He hit her, and she is in bad way. Very self-dangerous. Always when there is problem she is drinking too much. Too much, too much." He shook his head. He walked around the room nervously rubbing his stomach, then he opened our small refrigerator and took out a bag of espresso. "Okay, I'm gonna check her out. Then I make her drink some goddamn coffee."

I imagined John with his large, square hands, hands meant for the boxing ring. Ralph stirred, stretched his limbs, lifted his head to be scratched. I offered to go with Gunnar, but he wanted to go alone. Why had Dolores called Gunnar? Why hadn't she called her agent instead? I made some coffee, then fell asleep again before I could drink it.

Gunnar arrived back home two hours later with Dolores and several bags of matching black canvas luggage. Her face was tear-streaked, her eyes were red and puffy, her nose was swollen. Gunnar propped Dolores up against the wall, then dragged her luggage in. Once inside our door he put Dolores in a chair, steadied her head and rested her elbows on the table for ballast.

"I don't like how she is sounding."

"Where will she sleep?" We had no couch, no extra sheets or pillows.

Dolores and I shared the bed. Gunnar ran downstairs, brought up two piles of linen, slept on tablecloths spread out on the floor and used a stack of napkins for a pillow. Dolores was far from the ideal bedmate. She snored, and her breath was flammable.

Before dawn, Gunnar's large, hard, familiar body had crawled back into bed with us. He had left the floor full of table linen and was fast asleep with his arm around Dolores. I shook him.

He looked up at me, squinting with sleep, and then looked at Dolores waking up next to him.

"Hon-eee!" she smiled at him drunkenly.

He sat bolt upright and pulled the sheets around his chest.

"Jesu, I'm so tired, I'm like sleepwalker. Just I wake up on the floor and I'm thinking I fall out of bed so I get back in. I thought was you next to me."

"S'true," Dolores defended him sleepily, patting the muscles on his upper arm, then rubbing his chest. Overnight her eye had turned purple.

Dolores' familiarity with Gunnar's torso was troubling, but the better part of me wanted to forget about it and go back to sleep.

"Size forty breasts, a simple mistake—" I grumbled.

"Please, Kitchie, she is guest," he whispered.

"The bastard," Dolores wailed from under the sheets. "I could have him arrested. He's not supposed to use his hands, they're potential murder weapons. I should haul his ass into court, the son of a bitch. Bastard was fucking my co-star. Said he wasn't doing anything different than what I did for a living. He said that fucking wasn't a business, but it is," she wailed. "It's *my* business."

"All right, all right," Gunnar tried to shush her.

"And I *never* come when I'm on camera," she yelled, arguing with her lover in absentia. "And it ain't pussy," she continued to argue her point, "it's *drama*." She turned to Gunnar and wept at the unfairness of it all.

He held her against his body. They fit each other well.

"I'm sorry," he said, softly stroking her naked shoulder. "I'm sorry you got hurt. Nobody should be hurting nobody."

"He gave me his left. His *left*!" she carried on. "He could've killed me. I should get a lawyer."

"Harmon's got a cousin you'd love."

"Kitchie, please—" I had never embarrassed him before. "Get my pants," he appealed to my better side.

"*SONOFABITCH SHITFACED BASTARD!*"

If I had been our neighbor, I would have definitely called the police after a scream like that.

Before dawn, Gunnar was sheepishly ferrying coffee to both of us. I was feeling cranky and out of sorts, but Dolores seemed radiant. She was voluptuous, no angles, firm and perfectly molded like a big, ripe pear. I couldn't imagine how anyone wouldn't want to take a bite.

"Thanks, Champ." She hugged him sleepily as she took the coffee cup. Gunnar seemed nervous as she held him around his neck a little longer than a friend should. He undid her clasped hands.

Dolores walked around our apartment drinking her coffee, naked.

I pointed to her as she stretched and yawned, her bare ass to us, and shot Gunnar a what-are-you-going-to-do-about-this? look.

"Dolores, she is not . . . tame." He edged nervously out of the apartment with Ralph pulling him by the leash.

When he was gone, I spoke up.

"Dolores, put a towel on it."

"Listen, babe, I've got nothing you ain't seen before. And Champ's no stranger."

I paused for a moment.

"What does that mean?"

"That means what it means. You know what that means. We were an item."

I must have still looked confused because she added, "We were hot, get it? Before you, there was me."

I pulled my robe tighter around me.

She smoothed a flesh-colored cream over her cheeks.

"Guys never tell you the important stuff. Like Johnny. Of course, he hardly speaks English he's so goddamn dumb." She wiped her eyes, then, grudgingly, she wrapped the towel I'd thrown her around her body and blew her nose on the tip of it.

She opened her luggage and rustled through bags of makeup. In each bag were dozens of bulging sacs overflowing with cosmetics. The woman owned more mascara than Bloomingdale's. Dolores painted her face every day of her adult life in a slow, stubborn routine that hadn't altered through years of lovers and other disasters.

"Fucking eyelashes," she cried as two black caterpillars hung down the corner of each eye.

"How'm I gonna work like this? Shadows, bags, creases. I got a fucking black eye. Westmore himself couldn't fix me."

She returned to work with her mirror and brushes.

"I *gotta* stop this crying shit."

Dolores dabbed her eye with the ice pack Gunnar had made for her.

"I want to know about you and my boyfriend."

She sighed, slumped in the chair, and looked at me as though I was real. As real as the regret in her voice.

"Champ was the best thing ever happened to me, even though it wasn't the same for him like it was for me." She turned back to the mirror, carefully applied concealer over the bruise, and sipped her black coffee.

"I wanted something to happen with me and him, but it just didn't work out. Not that I didn't try. That money I loaned you? I figured he'd fuck up, then he'd owe me money, and you know how he doesn't like to owe nobody nothing, I figured he'd owe me and maybe I could collect once and a while a little, a little—You know, a little something. Just to stoke the coals, if you get my drift."

I was too angry to cry, but I cried anyway.

"Hey, what are you cryin' for? It was a calculated risk. The way he told it to me, I thought for sure you guys were going to go bust, just a crazy idea he had with some little cookie he had picked up. I was hoping it would all be over in a few months.

Sure, I was crazy about Champ, but he had other ideas."

I choked.

"Honey, button it. I told you, nothing happened."

When I wouldn't stop crying she said, "Christsakes, *I'm* the one with a black eye."

She had nothing to say after that. The room was so silent you could have heard a false eyelash drop. She held a small sable brush to her tongue and slowly licked it to a fine point. She dipped it thoughtfully into a gold vial.

She applied her eyeliner, straight, heavy and green.

"How'd a smart girl like you get involved with Champ?"

"The usual way." I blew my nose. "I fell in love."

"Yeah, or something."

She finished her toilette, dressed herself in a black jumpsuit, zippered her bags just as Gunnar came upstairs.

"You ready to go to work?" he asked. They were the same size, a good match, I thought, if a good match had been all he'd wanted.

"I'm a little shaky, honey." She looked up at him, an old lover who didn't need to say more than that to get his help.

"Okay, I drive you." I'd never thought of Dolores as being much more than an oversexed good sport. Now I had to think of her more viscerally.

I took the day off. I needed some time. I needed some air. I needed some information.

Frenchie lived on Saint Marks Place in a cellar apartment. I rang his bell and woke him up. He came to the gate rubbing his eyes, squinting in the sun like a mole. He was surprised to see me. He was wearing cream-colored silk pajamas with Pagliacci sleeves. The man dressed even for sleep. Except for a couch, there was no furniture. I looked around me; the entire apartment was furnished in clothes. Because it was a basement apartment, the ceiling of his living room, kitchen and small sleeping alcove were lined with plumbing pipes of every size and thickness, traveling in every direction. From these pipes were hung his extravagant and remarkable clothing collection. Tuxedos to beaded dresses, men's and women's clothes were everywhere, dripping down over our heads like stalactites. They made a curious decorative statement, functioning like curtains separating sitting and eating and sleeping areas.

Frenchie was considering taking a job with a vintage clothing store on Saint Marks Place. He searched through his rack of shirts, pulling out a lime-green silk and an old Hawaiian print.

"I'm tired of dressing The Babes. They're nice guys and all, but I'm getting too old for all that night work." He stood in front of the mirror, holding up one shirt and then the other.

"What're your options?" I asked, wondering if he was considering any other jobs.

"Between these two shirts? I'm definitely gonna wear the green one. Dress for success, remember that."

He offered me a soda, but I asked for tea instead. He opened up his fridge in which he apparently only kept Coca-Cola bottles.

"Hows 'bout I heat you up one of these babies?"

"I don't think so," I declined.

"Come on, hot with a little lemon, you'll never know what hit you."

"Fine."

"I love feeding women." He opened the fridge, felt bottle after bottle, feeling for the coldest one.

"Everything okay at the nest?" he asked cautiously. His face said he didn't want to know too much.

"I came to ask you about Gunnar and Dolores."

"Cat's out of the fry pan, huh?" His slow enunciation of words had a curious roundness. Without teeth, the human voice became guttural, slurry and primal.

"I suppose you knew all about Dolores?"

"You asking if I know Dolores, which you know I do, very well," he began cagily, "or you asking if I knew about her and Champ and how come it was I didn't say nothing about it to you before this?"

"I'm asking all those things."

"So, yes to the first two, and to the last one, because I'd known Champ for years already when you arrived new on the scene."

I listened patiently as he worked out his complex code of loyalty. "But the way I see it, it's okay for me to talk about Dotty and Champ because by now you're my friend too."

"So what was their relationship about?"

He raised his eyebrow at me. Was I stupid or something? "About?"

"Aside from sex, was there anything else between them aside from sex?"

"Champ knows you know?"

"He knows I know you know, and by now we all know I know," I assured him.

He chose a bottle, lined it up carefully with the checkerboard squares of his tablecloth, his movements as deliberate as his thinking.

"Champ know you're here?"

"He knows I'm not at work."

He fiddled noisily with the few pots under his sink, came out with a small, white, enamel one, uncapped the Coke, and poured it in. He saved one last sip in the bottle for himself and swigged.

"The way I see it, cars kiss cars, but even they're allowed to leave the scene of the crime."

He watched the soda boil and then he stirred the fizz down with a spoon.

"Yeah, well, okay. There was a glimmer of something in there for her, but only when it was over, if you ask me."

"Did she love him?"

"Listen, Dotty can't love nothing, especially if it's bigger than her fingernails. She's a drama queen, that's how come she got to be such a top pussy in those movies."

"And Gunnar?"

"He got out of it as fast as he could. It was like she was hanging on his neck, and he was saying real nice, please let go. He was very polite, he didn't want to hurt nobody's feelings."

"Then she did love—?"

"Nah. She was already hitting the mattress with Johnny Golden Gloves. She just couldn't let go. She wanted 'em both. You know how it is with a cock collector, no morals."

"Did you think it was right he borrowed money from her?"

"Hey, babe, if I counted up the right things in this world . . . well, what would be the point?"

He poured my hot soda for me.

"Rush from that'll sharpen your airwaves and tune you right in. Very vibrational way to start the morning, man. Fuck oatmeal, I mean talk about breakfast of champions—"

I listened to Frenchie slurp. I stirred my Coke.

"Champ," I mumbled disparagingly, pushing the boundaries

of Frenchie's loyalty about as far as it would go. "Why do you all call him that, anyway?" I asked quietly. My cup looked like a bottomless hole of black tar.

Frenchie smiled his toothless smile.

"Heyyy." Arms extended, chin lifted, he shrugged his shoulders at the obviousness of the answer. "What else you call someone who always comes up tops?"

It was almost midnight when I came home and found Gunnar was waiting up for me.

"Where have you been? Look, Kitchie, Dolores is back home. Apartment is empty, no luggage. You can check." He opened up our closet door, as though I would be relieved not to find Dolores hidden there.

"I don't care about Dolores," I frowned.

Discovering that Gunnar and Dolores had been lovers hadn't bothered me half as much as finding out he had taken her money under what I considered false pretenses. He had knowingly fed on her hope.

"What is wrong, then? I wait all day, all night. Not even a message you left. Is that nice?"

"Better not talk to me about nice. Why didn't you ever tell me about you and Dolores?"

"Why do you say you do not care about Dolores if you do care?"

He restrained himself and tried again. "Maybe I didn't want to explain. Maybe I thought you wouldn't like it very much."

"She loaned you money because she expected you to fail, and then she hoped you'd owe her a little nookie on the side."

"Hey, who said that?"

"She did. You knew how she felt about you, didn't you? You knew what she wanted, but you took her money anyway."

"She had enough to spare."

"Listen, your Aunt Magrid and the cookie jar was one thing, but this—"

"You are not fair," he protested.

"This isn't about fair, this is about *right*."

"Never am I unfaithful. Not once. There is no one but you."

"You took her money knowing that if we failed, the price of payback was outrageous." I was suspicious of that gangster streak. Just how immoral was he? How far would he go in the name of business and protecting his interests? Was I just another deal to dicker over? After two years, I still didn't know his trade secrets.

"You strung her along," I cried. "Are you stringing me along too?"

I thought about the past, I thought about the future. Two years ago, all I had wanted to do was cook, to live amongst pots and pans. All I thought I wanted was a little place with checkered tablecloths thrown over a few tables, a simple menu and the modest trimmings of a small-town life. Maybe I was a little crazy, but I wanted to feed people. It had been a long time since I had thought about the way I had once wanted things to be. I couldn't have those dreams back; still, I wanted to know what had happened to them. Gunnar had turned my dream into something big, more than I had ever expected, but not at all what I had meant. I owed him for the roller-coaster ride. Whether I had wanted it or not, I'd had success. Had the business of business eaten my dreams, or had they evaporated in the heat of the kitchen like a drop of water on a hot skillet?

"You took money from an ex-lover knowing Dolores expected you to fail and hoping she would have a hold over you."

"But we gave back. Is all paid up, with interest."

"Can't you understand? It's not the money, it's the *way* in which you took it."

Had Gunnar sold me out as artfully as he had Dolores? Had he fed on both our hopes?

"It's this whole thing with money you have—"

"Money is part of life," he insisted, "is nothing wrong with money. Is natural force, like weather."

"I'm not ungrateful, Gunnar, but it does change everything. Look at us, we have no life."

"You wanted to run gourmet soup kitchen, maybe?"

"When does this money-business thing stop? All we ever do is work. We never even take a vacation."

Then he mumbled a favorite Finnish proverb, one that I had heard before and had come to hate, "*Now the mouse reaches to the cheese plate.*"

The issues were starting to pop, our relationship cracking open like a leaky dam but with no little Dutch boy to plug up the holes.

"We got business, we must run it."

"I want to run it a little less and live a little more."

He was silent. He leaned against the wall and drummed his fingers on it, contemplating something for a minute. When he looked at me, hurt had settled in his eyes. I had wounded him.

Here it was, then. The mouse was at the cheese plate, the jig was up, do or die, jump and swim.

"I hate what you did with her."

"The sex was nothing, was before you—"

"I don't mean the sex. You let her think that we were going to fail. You knew what she wanted, what she'd expect. And you knew you were leading her on. And all for money."

He seemed confused, and hurt. "I did this for us."

I started to cry. He didn't get it. He didn't know what I was talking about.

We had come to that dark, bottomless place that couples know. The immovable impasse. The hole neither person knows how to climb out of.

From then on, neither one of us knew what to expect from the other. Lovemaking went on hold. Neither could afford to want the other in bed, too afraid of what it might cost. We had gone from clinical sex to passionate sex to no sex at all.

We relied on other forms of relating that were more basic than sex or talk, more to the point. We fought. We fought all the time. We fought over everything. We fought over sharpened pencils, blankets, pillows, cake frosting, coffee beans, spatulas, employee schedules, table settings. We fought over who put what where. We fought in the restaurant and in the apartment. We fought when the lights were on and when they were off, behind closed doors and out in the open in front of our staff. We lost our tempers every day. Every hour there was another issue worthy of venting our mutual spleens. And we didn't care who saw it. When Danny Boy criticized us for having arguments in the kitchen, I saw red. Red as beets, red as squab liver. I could have skinned him like a hunk of venison. I grabbed him by the buttons of his chef coat and looked into his face.

"Listen, you little shit," I exploded, "you try living your personal life in a restaurant morning, noon and night, and we'll see how well *you* do."

Fourteen

A little schmear of Moonstone, maybe?" Shalom reached into his paint-splattered overalls and offered me a succession of color chips as though we were playing a poker game. The dining room was scheduled to be painted, and I had to choose a color. A short, stocky man, Shalom sipped sugary tea while we looked over his color charts in the dining room. His unlit cigar dangled precariously from his lips.

"Creamy? You say you want it more creamy? So try Warm Ivory."

"Too pale, too dry," I countered, the old painting student rising up in me.

"Maybe you like Abbey Frieze instead?"

"Not warm enough, too gray."

"I am suggesting now a color that is beautiful yet so warm it's hot. Have a look-see at this Melon Moonlight."

There was something of the door-to-door salesman in Shalom's persistent but impatient patience.

"Not enough glow. We want people's faces to look *good* in here," I said.

"You never heard of pink light bulbs?" Shalom asked incredulously. He rattled off a list of other restaurants whose color problems he had solved in this manner, but soon he saw that this solution was lost on me.

Gunnar joined us. Gunnar had liked the old color, Dusty Rose.

"Why change?" he asked. "Old paint is still fine."

"It's too dark," I said.

"Every year a new color," Gunnar muttered.

"Things change."

Shalom interrupted our argument.

"Listen, children, don't argue. Listen to an old man. Paint the walls white and get pink light bulbs."

Both of us remained unmoved.

"Look, let me explain you something." His head shook in profound understanding of our plight, and he drew us nearer to him by leaning across the table.

"I'll schmear a few colors on the wall. Whatever colors you want and—" He sat back suddenly in his chair with great satisfaction. "And then, you'll see!"

His cigar butt had a life of its own as it wiggled happily from one side of his mouth to the other. "You'll look in the morning, you'll look in the night, you'll look, and you'll decide. Otherwise this is costing you plenty because the clock is ticking dollar bills."

I chose twelve different shades and insisted that Shalom paint them onto three different sides of the room. "So I can see how the color changes in the light," I explained.

Shalom smiled beneficently. "The customer is always right."

Gunnar disappeared back into his office where he busied himself with stacks of papers from Steve Krokadopolos and the

Laundromat Couple. He had encouraged other offers too from the Tillman family, who wanted a Kittridge's concession in their department store, and a soap opera star who wanted a boat cafe. While Gunnar contemplated percentages, square footage and profit margins, I waited for Diana Devine to show up to discuss the details of her twenty-fourth anniversary party.

Generations of good breeding had given Diana a thorough-bred jaw and kept her thin. Diana was a woman who cared about everything that went into her. Spritzers, please, nothing domestic, with a slice of lemon and lots of ice. She avoided the sun, her skin was cream, no peaches. She stayed on top of every new medical breakthrough for hair, teeth and body. She ate no animal fat, no eggs, and she knew pasta was good for her. She was known for her love of fashion and her legendary good works. Her husband was the fourth generation to run his family's publishing business. The couple were frequently mentioned in society gossip columns and were seen in the company of politicians, writers and European designers. Although it was a year away, there was talk of the President attending the Devine's twenty-fifth anniversary, already booked at the Waldorf.

I was still contemplating the effect of afternoon light on Oyster Pink as Kittridge's walls filled up with swatches of Alabaster, Cantaloupe, Princess Pink and Bermuda Beige when Diana Devine arrived with her anniversary entourage. Diana's grown daughter Dibbi had a round, polished face that still recalled childhood. Her body was a size larger and more robust than her mother's. She was blonde and blue-eyed and wore a more youthful Krizia to Diana's Valentino. Diana's son Toby looked like a boarding-school boy let out on holiday. His eyes darted every which way, falling first on the liquor behind the bar, then on the windows and front door, searching for escape hatches. He couldn't seem to decide what trouble to get into first.

Diana had also brought along someone known as KDB.

"Who is Kay Deebee?" I asked discreetly.

"Initials," Diana whispered. "One doesn't know, but one doesn't ask."

"She's a floral artist, her major work is with balloons," Dibbi added wisely.

"The children and I love the room, of course," Diana explained, "but we feel that it ought to be dressed up a bit. KDB is just a sensation at this kind of thing. We use her for that look one wants."

"She's like a member of the family, almost," offered Dibbi.

The balloon artist had one of those small, tightly wound Irish faces, like a clock bomb about to go off. She had streaked her natural blonde hair with green and wore it pinned up for that haven't-brushed-it-since-the-night-before look. She wore black lace tights, a fake cowhide dirndl skirt, fringed shawl and red cowboy boots with spurs and a red rose at her belt. This was not a woman interested in blending in. Her livelihood was predicated on originality. Hired to prettify and thematize society parties, KDB understood what the rich wanted. She had no desire to be in the fold, because she had done the fold one better: she had set its style.

KDB's clients hired her to design charity benefits, dinner parties, social events. Her work had been chronicled widely in fashion magazines. Obtaining KDB's services was a little like hiring Marcia the Magical Moose for adults: party favors from Tiffany, gold-covered almonds in small silver baskets, table and chairs wrapped in diaphanous Clarence House fabric, floral centerpieces fashioned from edible nasturtiums and sugar-dipped yellow roses, plastic slipper champagne glasses. The bill for the balloon artist's services would be astronomical, costing more than the dinner at Kittridge's.

KDB's lowly balloon assistant, Jonathan, whose job it was to carry balloons of every shape, size and color, followed her close by as she looked at our mottled walls, crinkled her nose, and gasped, "Oh, my God. This is *the look*. Fabulous. Tell me this man's name."

Shalom looked up from his paint cans to see who it was she might be talking about.

"I love it, but can you do it all over? Right up to the ceiling? Look Jonathan, it's froufrou camouflage. Peace fatigues. Of course the pastels should be a little deeper and all over, don't you think?"

"All over?" Shalom worried he was suddenly taking orders from two crazy women now. "Listen, I didn't want to do it on three walls, and now *this one* has me doing it all the way up to the ceiling?"

"You must give me your card. I always have jobs for talented people—"

"I should give you my card? I don't even want *this* job I'm getting so crazy from it, how should I want yours?"

While KDB cased the dining room for aesthetic defects and balloon opportunities, Jonathan took notes.

Diana anxiously tapped her lips with her long fingers. "It's an absolutely *mad* time for us." She confided the news of the Devine family: Donald's mother's eighty-fifth was to be held in Boca, Dibbi's engagement party was underway. Diana continued on as though I knew everyone in their family. The rich, in their kindest moments or their most self-serving ones, always had the grace to pretend that those who serviced them were really part of their inner circle. They swept you into their folds of privilege. Then they told you what they wanted you to do for them.

"So, you see, we're in for an absolute onslaught, so when I thought Kittridge's I thought, well, all right, *small and informal*. Of course discretion is a must. No newspapers, et cetera?"

"We're not in the gossip business," I reassured her.

"I ought not to have asked, of course. But with a guest list such as this, one feels one must ask. Now, a few minor points. The menu. Lamb, definitely. And that goat cheese lasagna thing, we hear it's marvelous, but is it messy? I want nothing people can't manage on a fork. No stringy melted cheese." She arched her eyebrow like a schoolmarm. "And no palate cleansers, too pretentious."

"They went out with the Tyrannosaurus rex," I agreed.

"And the dessert. Now, the children have their heart set on a cake, but I am quite at sea on sweets and endings."

We settled on lemon sorbet and a four-tier anniversary cake.

Gunnar walked back into the dining room in time for me to introduce him to Diana. The Devines were celebrating twenty-four years of being rich together, and Gunnar and I were trying to hold it together for one more day, our home was in shambles, the future of our business unknown. He took my elbow and walked me over to the bar.

"Who is this maniac?" he hissed, pointing to the strange vision that was KDB inspecting our dining room, followed by Jonathan, balloons bobbing.

"KDB, this is my partner Gunnar Gunnarson."

Partner, that ambiguous term. Maybe business, maybe love.

"Ah, yes, rack of sacrificial lamb, poinsettias, the hope of Easter." She turned to her assistant to finish her thought.

"It all would fit together so fabulously well with those pink guerilla walls."

"Was nice to meet you too." He turned to walk back into his office.

KDB gave off an energy that burned like smoke from a diesel. With her eyes closed, she paced the perimeters of the dining room, feeling the bar, tables and chairs with her fingers. She stood for a long time addressing the ceiling and the floor by waving her arms at them and breathing deeply.

"Silver." She spoke. "I see silver here." She spun around with her arms folded and looked Diana Devine square in the eyes. "I see it here, here and here, but over here," she pointed above the bar, "I see ultramarine. Deep, long-lasting blue." She folded her arms again, leaned against the table. "Di, love, do you see it?"

My place was to wait quietly by the door until this was over. I was suddenly filled with compassion for poor Shalom, quietly painting his samples in the hopes that his client would make up her mind. The three women went into a huddle that moved amoebically along the room, stopping at points KDB planned to change or decorate.

"Of course there'll be more than fifty," I overheard Diana. "CZ is flying in from Aspen and Brooke from Paris. I mean I couldn't very well stop them, could I?" she asked KDB.

"Everyone will blend. I'm ordering smaller chairs, silver bamboo, and we'll have at least ten to a table. That'll take care of seventy, don't you think?" KDB turned to me.

"Seventy?" I gulped.

"Give or take five here or there."

"That's way over my fire code."

'I can't very well change restaurants now. I only hope I can stop it at eighty," Diana said helplessly. "As soon as everyone heard about it, they started calling and making plans to fly back from all over the place. It's so sweet, really, but so . . . so unexpectedly problematic. It was supposed to be a little get-together and now it's a bloody behemoth."

Dibbi took her mother's arm and sat her down. KDB pushed me into the kitchen. "Don't mind Di. She and Donald have been talking divorce lately. Everyone's coming to this thing to cheer them on one more year."

I brought out a pot of restorative tea on a tray with several cups and saucers.

Diana blew her nose and turned to her daughter helplessly. "I mean, how do you say no to Henry Kissinger?"

There was a sudden explosion of helium balloons bursting all over the dining room. I heard the door to Gunnar's office bang open as he ran in to my side.

"Sorry," apologized Jonathan as he explained. "A few of our number-two latex popped—"

"Walls look like zebras, and now we got balloons all over," Gunnar whispered. "How we are opening up for service tonight?" He left me to fend for myself with the balloon artist.

"Okay, Kitchie, bottom line, I need five tables of twenty," KDB told me.

"We can't feed twenty at the same table. This is a restaurant, not a mess hall," I explained.

"Listen, these people love a tight squeeze once in a while. Being manhandled is an entertaining departure from the rest of their life where everyone's kissing their ass."

She underscored her point dramatically by popping every balloon she'd brought but the two silver and blue ones she had chose for the Devines' party. Gunnar stayed in his office this time, but Shalom jumped at the explosions, splattering some more paint on his overalls.

KDB turned to her assistant. "Jonathan, you must get that man's card. He has an incredibly profound understanding of color."

Sunday morning, the day of the Devines' party, Ralph woke me up with an urgent lick on the face. He needed a walk. It was a freezing-cold morning. The heat hadn't gone on yet, and as I looked through the frosty windows, everything outside promised to be even colder. Six A.M., the day still dark, the outside world barely moving.

A new snow had fallen overnight and covered the old snow. Ralph and I crunched along. A bread truck rolled lumberously down the street; behind it a taxicab teetered uncertainly between the mushy snow banks. Ralph looked young again as he scampered back into our building when his walk was over. Instead of returning to the apartment, I brought Ralph with me into Kittridge's. I unleashed him to wander while I caught up on some work. Ralph loved to sniff the kitchen floor for whatever tidbits he could find there, hoping to fill his belly. He circled the kitchen, near the wine room, his dog tags jingling vigorously. He must have found something really good, I thought, probably some loaves of stale bread. I didn't think about the dog again until he settled lazily by my legs, leaning on my shoes, sighing because his picnic was over.

The Devines' party was on everyone's mind. The tension mounted, nerves were raw. The secretary had dropped off the guest list and place cards. These were the names you saw on museums, libraries and hospitals. Not the names on little brass plaques above elevators, either; these were the people for which entire wings and pavilions were named. Everyone wanted to do a good job. Able arrived at work two hours early. Wasabe showed up with special ceremonial knives. Valentine worked feverishly but fumed with disapproval as Danny Boy called home to read the impressive guest list to his parents. "The rich don't know how to eat," Valentine ranted as he carved the racks of lamb with frightening speed and accuracy.

Shalom arrived to do touch-ups on windowsills, door frames and moldings. He assured me the latex paint would be dry by that afternoon. Able had made lunch, and we had invited Shalom to eat with us.

"How you like this, Shay-loam? Better than that borscht and chicken soup you people are always eating?"

"I could eat like this for the rest of my life."

"Well, hell, eat some more, then," Able commanded.

"You're killing me," said Shalom, "but don't stop, I love it!"

It was the most relaxed part of the day, until the pastry chef came into the dining room. His face was white, drained of color. At first, I thought it was flour. Then I thought he was sick. Then I realized he was furious. In fact, I had never seen him so angry. He looked like he was going to quit.

"Someone," he looked directly at me, "or *something* has eaten my cake."

"What cake?"

He looked at me like I was an imbecile.

"There is only one cake. Tonight's cake. The Devines' anniversary cake. The piece de resistance. *The end of the meal*. What cake . . . " He mumbled on in incoherent rage.

"A four-tier cake for one hundred people. A great big chunk bitten out of every layer, like some animal. Even if I *could* make it again, where would I get the raspberries? Australian berries in February—" He turned to Shalom for comfort and understanding.

"So," his tone was suddenly acid. "What do you want me to do about it? Start all over again with *frozen* berries?"

Guiltily, I remembered Ralph's dog tags jingling as he searched the floor of the quiet kitchen, his satisfied sigh as he snuggled up against my legs earlier that morning. I remembered now that the baker had placed the Devines' cake in the wine room after he'd assembled it. It was too big for any refrigerator, and so he had placed it in the cool wine room so that the butter cream frosting would hold its shape overnight. The door had been mistakenly left ajar, and Ralph must have nosed his way in.

For this, our showdown argument, Gunnar and I moved upstairs to our apartment. This was the big one. He wanted to blame, and I wanted to accuse.

"You let *dog* into wine room to eat cake? You want to kill restaurant?"

I stormed around our living room, then yanked my boots on.

"I'm sick of the restaurant!" I cried.

"Hey, I gave you what you wanted. Now you are sick of it?"

I shoved my hair into a woolen hat and pulled it down over my ears.

"Where are you going?"

"I'm getting out of the way of your success."

I struggled angrily into my coat and tied a scarf around my neck.

"*I* don't let dogs eat cake," he said.

"Meaning?"

"What do you *want*? What in Jesu shit fuck Christ to hell do you want?"

"I want my life back," I yelled. And I meant it.

He bellowed a stream of Russo-Finnish invective, and Ralph, worried, trotted over to lick him reassuringly. Gunnar did not exactly receive the animal with open arms but, rather, raised his leg karate-style, kicked the dog, and sent him careening clear across the room, squealing in surprise and pain.

The next thing I knew, I was out the door with Ralph who immediately forgot his brush with death and happily wagged his tail, following all the way down the stairs of the building, only too pleased to be getting another walk this morning. He looked like he was smiling.

"Oh, shut up, stupid," I said when we got outside.

From a dog's point of view, it had been a stellar day. Ralph had eaten an entire wedding cake and pissed in clean snow, twice.

Fifteen

I needed time to think. Something was over, but I wasn't sure yet what it was. I felt in my pocket. Ginger had given me the key to her apartment years ago, and I still carried it on my key ring. The day was coming to a surprisingly gentle end for a brooding February afternoon. The wind had died down, and the air had warmed enough to soften the snow. The day had split itself into two seasons as winter yielded to the balmy promise of an early spring.

I waited thirty minutes before a taxi driver stopped, one who was sympathetic to dogs. Santiago Oliviero # 534 DJ generously agreed to take us to the Upper West Side to Ginger's apartment. During the ride he discussed all the dogs that had ridden in his cab. He was also eloquent on the subject of the abandoned animals he had saved, or scraped, off the FDR. My path had been crossed by a good Samaritan. For the moment, things were looking up.

Santiago Oliviero left me off at a four-story town house. Ginger had a small studio on the third floor at the back of the building. I didn't have the key to Ginger's lobby door, which was locked. I wrote a quick note and stuck it above her bell.

Overhead, dark grey clouds had gathered quickly, and within

minutes I was a wet pilgrim holding onto a barking dog who, frightened by thunder, strained fiercely at the leash and pulled me along quickly to nowhere. Life had drenched me. The snow was pockmarked by rain bullets, the melting banks gushed into the gutters like urban brooks. Everything was washing away, the structure of my life was dissolving. At the beginning of the end of winter, I was overcome by a premature spring rain, as I had once been by Gunnar's love. I thought of my childhood when love and food were so meanly portioned out in frozen cubes of TV dinner. I thought of the blind gourmet, so cruelly set in his pursuit of perfect taste, and I thought of Gunnar, the man in my corner of the ring.

I looked for a building lobby that was open. A doorman let me in to the large apartment house across the way. I thanked him, and we exchanged notes on the storm. I sat down on a lobby armchair and fell asleep. Ralph rested his head on my feet and snored contentedly. It had been a baptism of sorts, a perfect way to begin a personal revolution.

"Trouble in paradise, huh?" Ginger had found my note and come looking for me.

"You were my last hope at long-lived relationships," she sighed as we climbed the stairs to her studio apartment. She unlocked the door and took my coat.

"Make yourself at home and sit down."

"On what?"

Her mismatched dining-table chairs, one chrome, two wood, one rattan, were covered with unfolded laundry. She scooped more clothes off her couch, a Woolworth's fold-up foam thing, purchased after her divorce. She held the pile in her arms, looked around, and transferred it onto her bed. The clothes read like a fabric diary of her last week's activities. A bodysuit worn at her last Nautilus session, dancing shoes, a red party dress, sweaters for work. She stuffed some clothes in the filing cabinet. I felt completely at home.

Ginger's only window looked out onto a brick shaftway. She had never bothered to hang a curtain or venetian blind. My excuse for domestic inadequacy had always been lack of time; Ginger blamed DNA.

"My mother couldn't hang curtains either," she explained. "It's the gene pool."

A stack of interior design magazines by her bed were piled so high she used them as night tables and positioned her mismatched reading lamps on them. Her showplace was her bathroom, or rather, its contents. Ginger took great care of her skin, hair and teeth. It wasn't just vanity that moved her, it was her need for ritual. Her shelves were a jumble of beauty machines, skin steamers, hair dryers, lotions, tonics and creams of every color and for every purpose. Not that Ginger wore much makeup. It was all the stuff that was applied before the makeup that held her interest. Like the rest of her apartment, it was all about preparation.

Ginger had to move her car, and as we both got in, she turned to me and said, "Want some pizza?" What I really wanted was to see the party at Kittridge's. If Ginger would drive me downtown past the corner where it stood, I could look into the restaurant's large, open windows.

"Can't you stay away from there?" she asked.

"I need closure," I explained.

"Talk about addictive behavior. Maybe you should consider one of the twelve-step programs."

"How very social worker of you. Now, drive on, Jeeves."

Ginger brought us downtown. The streets were still wet from the rain, and the city had a quiet, washed quality. There were very few people out, and by the time we reached the waterfront, the streets were deserted.

The car rounded the corner.

"Okay, *now*," said Ginger. I slid down to the floor of the car, and, leaning on the passenger seat, I peered out over the window.

"I feel like a goddamn idiot hiding this way," I said.

"Well, that should tell you something."

The scene through Kittridge's large front window was like too many fireflies locked inside too small a jar, unable to fly around but furiously working their lights. The men were tuxedoed, the women wore designer dresses and carefully coiffed hair.

"Oh, my God," Ginger exclaimed. "Look, look! It's Kissinger! I'm parking. This I have to see." She searched her glove compartment. "Where the hell are the binoculars when you need them?"

There must have been over one hundred people in Kittridge's that evening. The high ceilings were covered three feet thick in bobbing blue-and-silver helium balloons. The ordinarily spacious room was congested with flower arrangements, more balloons, tassels, and the whole length of the bar had been wrapped in the same opalescent satin that also covered the tables. High silver candelabra were affixed to sculpted twists of barbed wire, sprayed gold.

"Talk about traffic jams," Ginger whistled.

I wondered where people were going to sit until I saw where

they did sit. The balloon artist had gotten her way. There were five long tables, and at each one, twenty famous, wealthy human beings sat shoulder to shoulder, crushing their Armanis and Valentinos. As soon as they were seated, the waiters appeared carrying dishes. Since there was no space between people or tables for waiters to serve the food, each dish was given to those seated at the end to be handed down the rest of the table. I squinted in disbelief as I watched one guest hand the dish to the next all the way down the line of the table. The dishes were hot and people shook their burnt hands. One woman experienced a slurp of gravy fall into her lap. She stood as a waiter tried to reach her with what I assumed was a napkin doused in club soda.

I felt sick. "Let's go."

At that moment, Gunnar came out of the kitchen to survey the scene. He stood behind the bar, slumped against the cash register, and folded his arms across his chest. With his arms crossed, he appeared to be barely holding himself up while the white kitchen rag in his hand waved like a flag of surrender.

"The night is young," said Ginger, revving up her engine. "Want me to circle around a second time?"

"No." As far as I was concerned, the party was over.

Was it any consolation that if my heart was more or less broken, Gunnar's was probably smashed into smithereens? Had he picked the right woman but done the wrong thing? Loved generically but not specifically? Was it all the fault of some stray business gene that had failed to yield to love?

I stayed with Ginger for two days. It was all that either one of us could stand. Her home was too much like mine; it made me homesick to be there. Besides, she had mice.

Lilly was away in Europe on a buying trip, so I returned to her apartment where I'd grown up. Its warm, wine-colored walls welcomed me. Though most of Lilly's collection was kept in a bank vault, the apartment was still crammed with art. In my old room, where once there had been a dollhouse and toys, paintings were piled like artistic bramble, overtaking my childhood space, replacing me like siblings.

I camped out on the couch with Ralph, stayed in the living room, used the phone, cooked for myself in the old kitchen, stuffed the refrigerator with more food than I could ever eat. A Delft clock mounted on the living-room wall ticked and tocked, its pendulum swinging peacefully and evenly.

Frenchie showed up unexpectedly, to deliver a few of my things from my apartment.

"How did you know I was here?" I asked.

"Champ told me."

I hadn't spoken to Gunnar in days, but it was just like him to consider my options and know exactly which one I would choose. It was chess. Gunnar and I stayed proud and silent at the opposite sides of the board while the rest of the pieces in our court visited back and forth, like advance troops.

"This is some place," Frenchie whistled. "You grew up here? Looks more like a museum than a home."

This from a man who lived in a clothes closet.

I spent the next few days in the hands of a lawyer who suggested contractual negotiation. The verdict was, I couldn't just walk off. Either I sued or countersued or Gunnar and I worked out an equitable agreement by which we terminated our corporation. Who needed a wedding? This was as close to divorce as you could get without the complications of marriage.

Gunnar called by the end of the week.

"So? You are coming back to work?"

As long as I kept thinking of our relationship as business, I would have to follow those rules. But I hadn't just been in business. I had been in love, which called for other rules.

"You want to leave me?" He seemed shocked and hurt.

"I want to leave Kittridge's."

"Shit," he said. He was used to making deals that went his way.

"You are scared, Kitchie?"

"Sure, I'm scared to leave, but I'm more scared to stay."

"Shit to hell. Where you are going?"

"Where I should have gone in the first place. Or at least where I should go now. Someplace small—"

"Leaving rat race, right? Someplace warm? Florida, maybe? Grapefruits and lemons, right? I like Florida. I like oranges." He kept hinting, hoping I'd invite him along. I wouldn't, even though I still loved him.

"I don't know," I said quietly, "I haven't decided yet."

"You want small seasonal business? Slow winter, busy summer? How about we do Summer Kittridge's together." I remembered the first time I saw him, leaning back on his chair, shaded by his hat. He was still roping in his steer. I thought of the time we stopped on the turnpike, coming home from Provincetown. We had both been intoxicated by the scent of business love. He had been so forthright, and I had been so willing.

"You're welcome to the business, Gunnar. You'll have to buy me out, but I won't stand in the way of you having it." He had some hard decisions to make. In some ways, harder to make than mine.

"Now *I* am scared," he said. "Goddamn combinations of two peoples together is impossible!" There was a long pause as he regrouped. "You got me over goddamn love barrel. Jesu Christo, small town, *where* you say you going to?"

We achieved that classic state known to couples as the stand-off, only we lived it through business details. For the next two weeks, we spoke on the phone and met at Kittridge's every day. I signed papers, bank statements, deposits and various legal, bank and tax documents. I removed more things from the apartment.

Each day, Gunnar had meetings with people I'd never seen before and phone calls from names I didn't recognize. When two men showed up wearing expensive suits and alligator shoes, I asked Gunnar who they were, but he wouldn't tell me, nor would he introduce me.

"You don't need to know those men." He strong-armed me with his answer.

"I *want* to know."

"You are suddenly so interested in business you are leaving?"

"The point is, I'm still your partner."

"Point is, you are not in my bed at night."

He had that madman-moving-mountains look.

I stopped going to the restaurant. I contacted my lawyer, and we set in motion all the necessary papers to sell the business to Gunnar. Gunnar called me at Lilly's, surprised and hurt when he received the papers, though not unwilling to go through the legalities. I had the impression that buying the business fit right into his larger plan. I could have pushed him harder to tell me what he was doing, but the time was right for growing a space between us. I found out soon enough, anyway. Able, the kitchen mole, leaked the goods. Gunnar intended to sell the restaurant to a group of backers who were intending to move Kittridge's uptown. They would disassemble the bar, gut the premises, and reconstruct the interior uptown in a space two or three times the original size. An architect had already drawn up plans. They were due to start construction as soon as I signed the papers. I tried to imagine Kitchie's being taken apart, piece by piece, reassembled like a child's erector set. Gunnar hadn't wanted me to know, afraid I'd renege on the deal.

Gunnar intended to buy my share of the restaurant for notes. He would pay me a monthly sum off the top of his profits from the new restaurant. It was a fair amount, and I thought I could manage reasonably on it, with enough money to start something else of my own. We continued to see each other for business purposes, but we were as distant as two people who love each other can be.

While the lawyers worked out the details, Gunnar told me over dinner that he intended to sell Kittridge's to his backers in exchange for fifty percent ownership of an uptown location.

"You're going to sign it over before you sign a lease to an uptown restaurant?"

"Sure. Is like collateral."

"So, you used our restaurant to buy your own restaurant?"

"Hey, just say word, and you are my partner again. I am on fast track now."

He was like one of Chagall's flying men, head all twisted around, rootless and floating, blown by dybbuk winds into a fairytale sky.

"You will see, Kitchie, I will prove I can have big success without you."

"I have no doubt you are going to prove something," I said. Gunnar never said he missed me, but I knew he could not sleep without me.

In three days we were due to meet in my lawyer's office and sign the papers. He was in Chicago, at another one of his business meetings. I was in Lilly's kitchen, eating a sandwich and reading a book when Able called me.

"Get your drawers on, Kitch, big old critic from *Chic!* is on the books for tonight. Thought you'd want to know. I'm sick as a dog, and Val's in charge. Can you come down?"

Restaurant critics don't announce themselves, but, then, Lefty Lieberman was no ordinary critic. Lefty was a man of letters who had interviewed everyone from Einstein to Picasso. Now, in the twilight of his career, he wrote about style and food in his column "What's New Now" for *Chic!* magazine. A man who had eaten with kings might be trusted to know a thing or two about dining out. I wanted to meet the great Lefty Lieberman. Besides, a good review from *Chic!* would only make Kittridge's more valuable. I could renegotiate my deal with Gunnar and end up with more money for my own business.

I worked the front that evening and shook hands with stout, bald Lefty who walked slowly to his seat, leaning on an ivory walking stick. He wore a purple sweater, purple tie and purple socks. When he removed his hat, he replaced it with a colorful beanie designed to cover his bald spot and keep his head warm. As soon as he and his three friends had sat, he unfolded his napkin and tied it around his collar like a bib. It was his signal for the waiter to bring the menu. He ordered, then began to watch us, his arms folded over his chest like an Indian chief.

I brought the order into the kitchen and gave it to Valentine who frowned at the dupe.

"VIP," I said.

"No one should have this much power," Valentine carried on.

"It's the American way, old buddy," Danny Boy agreed, imitating Able in absentia.

"Bad enough we have the politicians to tell us how to live, here we have the critics too. Critics to tell the rich where to eat," he added disgustedly. It was the peculiar irony of Valentine's career that the greater his skill, the wealthier his clientele.

"And from a magazine for the vain and the rich, no less," he continued.

There were already eight dupes hanging up at Valentine's station. The papers looked like storm flags warning of choppy seas.

"Jump the dupe, Val," I ordered. "This is important."

Valentine snorted. Was that the rumblings of Vesuvius I heard?

I knew from his reviews that Lefty liked his food hot, his bread crusty, his sausage spicy. He did not like too sweet a dessert, and he liked to taste off his guests' plates. His friends were in high spirits, out to enjoy Kittridge's. All we had to do was get the food to him on time and hot.

It was the busiest part of the evening. The dining room had become a track meet with waiters running back and forth to bring orders into the kitchen and carry out food to bring to tables. I felt winded with excitement, but nervous. I started in on the checklist. Was Lefty's bread hot enough? Were the butter ramekins wiped neatly along the edges? Had the silver been checked on Lefty's table? Did they have enough water? Did they need another round of drinks? Had the bathrooms been spot-checked? I was nervous, being back at Kittridge's and working the floor. It was clear that the kitchen was slow and the food was taking too long. We had a full house and customers had begun to complain. Twenty minutes had gone by since I had taken Lefty's order, and there was still no food on his table.

I slipped into the kitchen and saw that Valentine had not started cooking for the table. Even if he started now, it would be another fifteen minutes before the table saw food.

"I told you to jump the dupe!"

MG had joined me in the kitchen. As he slid past me he said, "Whatever you do, don't give them any more bread and water, they've starting making prison food jokes."

The atmosphere in the kitchen was charged with negative ions.

"Start that table *now*, Val," I ordered.

It mattered to Valentine not just what he cooked, but who he cooked for. We had ideological differences. He couldn't keep politics out of food. He could not be loyal to me without being untrue to himself.

He began to mutter to himself, slam the doors of the coolers and the stove. Danny Boy put out the appetizers, increasing the pressure on Valentine to finish the entrees. An interior time bomb was ticking. He snorted and stamped behind his station, his nostrils flaring like a horse straining at the bit.

I would not leave the kitchen now, and kept my eyes on Valentine.

MG came back into the kitchen to report. "The first course is a big hit."

Valentine's face was beet red from heat or anger or both. He was snorting like a captured beast, banging pots and shoving pans along the range. First he threw a dish, then a knife. He tore his apron off. He left the station, ran downstairs, out the kitchen, out the door, out the restaurant. Slam.

Danny Boy looked at me in disbelief. "Val's leaving?"

"Looks like," I answered, already reaching for an apron.

"Who'll cook the food?"

"Move over," I said and took a long swig of ice water.

Valentine was true to himself, and so, at last, was I. I had taken hold again of the best part of what I had started with Gunnar. I had reclaimed what I had always loved.

I was overdue for another cosmic look-see, if Slav could spare the time. His hotline, 212 ASTROFON, had proven so successful that now Slav was the star of his own show on cable television. He sat at a desk in front of a dark constellar map that set off his gleaming white hair. He appeared positively stentorian as he took callers' birth dates and, with the aid of a computer, interpreted their astrological strife. It didn't surprise me that Slav could no longer make house calls, but it was heartening that he took care of me over the phone, for old times' sake.

"I've been thinking about you," he said. "The aspects being what they are, I'm not at all surprised you called. I suppose you're feeling the effects of your Saturn return?" He sighed like a patient grandfather. "Sooner or later, it all comes out in the cosmic wash. It's just your natal makeup flaring up again. You'll be pushed in a new direction by the universe, pushed to your turning point. By my calculations, around the middle of the month." I heard him rustling through his ephemeris. At least he wasn't using his computer with me.

There was food all over my chart, gravy dripped from the points of my stars, and a constellation of pots, pans and spatulas would follow me wherever I went, whatever I did.

"But change is in the wind, Kitterina Kittridge," Slav cautioned. "This is your crossroads."

"I knew that already, Slav," I said, right before I hung up.

Sixteen

Kittridge's

If forks were awarded to restaurants on the basis of chutzpah, Kittridge's would surely deserve four. A gem of an old neigh-borhood bar located in the historic port of our city, evoking sea shanties, galleys, and doubloons, Kittridge's is worth a look, a taste, and a visit. Intrepid diners will find a taste of the Brave New World Cuisine at Kittridge's, where for starters one finds an ethereal tapioca soup so rich and garlicky it can only be en-joyed on this side of heaven's pearly gates. Other appetizers in-cluded a wonderfully coarse-textured rabbit terrine flecked with pistachios and rum-soaked golden raisins and a satisfy-ing, tangy blue cheese souffle.

Our chicken with four olives was a properly spiced and zesty entree, not too astringent or briny. A flavorful stew prepared with three different meats was served with a homemade noo-dle. An evocative boned quail stuffed with eggplant caviar and roasted yellow peppers and wrapped in grape leaves was plump and succulent, and a light tomato concasse made an artful sauce served over the accompanying orzo.

Kittridge's is the love child of two consenting adults, Kitterina

Kittridge and Gunnar Gunnarson. Their flair for the unusual is felt throughout the dining experience. From the rich mahogany interior to the menu's original combinations of flavor and texture, by whatever name you call it, this cathexis cuisine is right on target, borrowing freely from many countries yet speaking sensibly to the palate. The dishes here pull from a range of ethnic culinary traditions which are creatively combined and satisfyingly rendered. Two forks to Kittridge's. Bravo, Brave New World!

Rayburn Billy showed up with a copy of the review and a bottle of expensive champagne.

"Coals to Newcastle," he smiled as he threw Gunnar *Chic!* magazine.

"Now that someone's given you a reputation, Champ, you're going to have to live up to it."

"What is this New World Cuisine?" Gunnar asked cautiously, thumbing through the review.

"I don't know either, but you cook it," Rayburn smiled.

"And two forks, why not three?"

"Greedy, greedy," Rayburn warned.

"Sunday we all go celebrate, eat out three forks." He grabbed me. "Makes me hot just to think about it." We kissed, for old times' sake, as though love was still an everyday sensation. He gave me a pesto kiss, tasting of garlic and basil, someone else's food, I thought.

Slapping the table with both palms down, Gunnar made the noise of success. "We are on fucking map now!" Gunnar turned the imaginary handles of an imaginary motorcycle and revved up, "Vroom, vroom, vroom."

"Congratulations," my mother called the next morning, from Paris. Germany would be next on her buying tour, then Denmark, then back to Italy. She seemed surprised that a restaurant could actually attract Lefty Lieberman's attention.

"A lot of people actually *enjoy* eating," I explained. "They like reading about it too."

"I suppose. Of course, these days, even stereo speakers get reviewed in the newspapers." Like grape juice turned into wine, food had metamorphosed into something more than Lilly thought it deserved.

Frenchie came to celebrate too. He sat at our bar dressed in an impeccably vintage tux, a live advertisement for his new business, Threads. He handed his business cards to anyone who admired his clothes. Ginger and her new boyfriend, her field-work supervisor, sat alongside the resplendent Frenchie, drinking Rayburn's champagne. Dolores, in absentia, sent congratulatory orchids from South America, where her career was flourishing.

Wally and a very pregnant Fatima came bearing gifts, a painting of Kittridge's bar. "I'm getting so good, it amazes me," Wally said as he handed me the still-wet canvas. "The cerulean blue is what gets me, right here," he pointed to the left-hand corner of the painting. He admired his own work so tenderly, I hadn't the heart to disagree. I held little Wally on my lap, a little red-haired Egyptian clutching at his pull toy, a wooden beagle whose head shook every time he pounded it against the table.

"Quite the monster, wouldn't you say? Hands like Raphael, eyes the color of a Titian sky." Wally the family man, rewarded in this life with a fine son, a stipend from his rich aunt and a wife one week overdue with their second child.

If we were busy before, now we were packed. The phone rang so much that we installed two extra lines. The reservation book was full, the bar was stuffed, the kitchen was on overload, the whole staff high on success, low on energy. There was more business than even Gunnar knew how to handle comfortably. The tables turned so many times that the endless round of faces became a blur. I continued to work in the kitchen with the boys. Since Valentine had left, we had hired two young cooks, both women. Able, though still irascible, was on his best behavior ever since, in retaliation for some sexist remark, one of the new women threatened to cut off his balls with poultry shears. I continued setting the menus and specials, running the kitchen, and keeping my eye on the front of the house.

Gunnar's future partners were more eager than ever to expand uptown and into other cities, but with this kind of money coming in, there could be no disposing of Kittridge's, no gutting its interior and reconstructing it uptown in a space three times as large. Before the review, the wooden panels along one wall had been removed, measured, labeled, wrapped like modern mummies in bubble wrap, and set to rest in large wooden crates on their way uptown. After the review, Gunnar and I watched anxiously as carpenters unwrapped the panels and carefully nailed them back onto the walls where they belonged. Now that Kittridge's had taken its place among the city's busiest restaurants, the original Kittridge's would have to stay right where it was.

"Nobody is making hamburgers out of cash cow," explained Gunnar.

I was too tired to travel uptown to my mother's apartment each night. Instead, I would drag myself upstairs to our apartment to sleep. It didn't matter anymore whether Gunnar slept next to me. We were too tired to hiccup, let alone have sex or talk about why we weren't having it. So Ralph and I moved in again, for the sake of convenience. My return had no cathartic significance. Gunnar and I had become mere roommates. The only things we shared were business and the dog, who had taken up his old place at the foot of our futon. Downstairs during the day it was hello, goodbye, sign this, read that. We had finally emerged as business partners, pure and simple.

I didn't need a cosmic checkup to know that something wasn't right. My life had taken a detour, and I had gotten stuck somewhere I didn't want to be. What turn had I missed, and how would I find it again? Franklyn Mist, my old watercolor teacher, used to say that when you drew a tree, you also drew the empty space between the branches. "If you want to see what is," he said, "take a good, hard look at what isn't."

What I wanted wasn't about money. My mother had made plenty of it. I knew how to make it too. I had always known. I was as good at making money as Gunnar. He just wanted it more. Hungered after it so much that it never left his mind. It wasn't about cooking either, or success. It wasn't that I didn't value what we'd achieved. It had been a great ride, and I had gone a fair distance. But I had skipped a step, lost something along the way—not by falling in love with Gunnar, but by going into business with him. Gunnar had mastered the business of business, while I had lost my heart to it. The time had come to reclaim that sad little hunk of organ meat. Unless I wanted to end up like Lilly, selling the thing she loved best instead of making it.

Every meal I'd cooked for someone else had brought me closer to my own appetites, which, I realized now, had nothing to do with food but everything to do with love. Other people's hungers were shadows of my own. I had to recapture what I had lost. The best cooking didn't start in pots and pans, but in the heart.

I stayed on for three more months, until our success settled down and behaved itself. Finally, Gunnar was ready to sign his new deal. He had it all planned out. He would take care of expansion, while I kept the original Kittridge's going. He had come home one evening, after spending the day in Chicago. I had lost count of the number of days Gunnar had gone without sleep. The bounce in his step was gone, and he slumped under the weight of his upcoming deal. His eyes were so small and dark, you might have thought he was on something, though business was his only drug of choice. He took his shirt off; his striped banker's pants hung in tired folds. He rubbed his bare chest and drank a bottle of cold beer. If we'd had a table or a desk, Gunnar would have spread his papers on it, but he used the floor instead. Gunnar arranged his charts and projections as Ralph watched with interest. The rustling papers sounded a lot like potato chips, and the dog wanted to be ready should any be offered.

"I'm leaving," I said.

Gunnar looked up from his papers, then pushed them away. He was very quiet. Gunnar knew an ending when he heard one.

"Will you come back?"

"I don't know. It depends on what I find."

"I can change. Give me, at least, one more try."

"Ninety-day money-back guarantee?"

With desperate charm, he continued selling himself to me. It was hard for him to let me go. He was driven to extract profit from every human situation, even ones that were over. It was why I had fallen in love with him. He always came up on top because everything in a life worth living was worth exploiting, and everything worth having was a deal worth making.

"You have stopped loving me?" It was incomprehensible to him.

"This has nothing to do with love."

"Then, is not over between us?"

"I don't know. I don't know what we still have."

I had never heard fear in his voice before.

"I will give you Kittridge's. Just stay."

"You can't give me what is already mine." I smiled sadly, remembering the big wad of hundred dollar bills stowed securely in his hip pocket.

"We can get married."

I'd be marrying a business, when what I wanted was him.

"Ralph would eat the wedding cake, and I'd be in your way."

"You don't want to be with me anymore?"

"I don't want to be *in business* with you anymore."

He sat on the bed, then fell back onto it with the weight of his realization.

I knew he thought his plans were crushed. I also knew he'd have a new plan by morning.

"We made such great success together," he said, uncomprehending, close to tears.

Could I have hurt him any more if I had said I didn't love him?

We spent the night talking. Untangling the mess of strings that bound us, each knot attached to another. Love, ambition, money, until we had a long skein of what was right, what was wrong and what was, finally, forgivable. I left in the morning, with two bags and the dog, and started to drive, thinking I would head south, towards Miami or the Keys.

But in the end, I wanted to be somewhere cold, clean and crisp as apples. So I traveled up the east coast, stopping at any bed and breakfast that would take Ralph. Spring was in full blast. I spent a month riding the coast and walking along as many beaches as I could find until I came to Comfort Isle, a small island off the coast of Maine.

Comfort is not a glamorous island. Its beaches are not long and wide, but uneven, sparse and craggy. The coves are pebbly and rocky and thick with brush. The sand is coarse. The cliffs are steep and unclimbable. The trees are short and bend with the wind. There is scrub and tangled greens in place of forest.

It is hardly a place of luxury. People live here without a sense of plenty. There is one doctor, one pharmacy, a single gift shop, one ice cream store, a video arcade where parents park their adolescents. There is one grocery, one gas station and, on the other end of the island, a pizzeria, open Thursday through Sunday, that does not offer anchovies. The town's worn patina is part of its local pride. It is a complacent, restorative place.

The houses are small gingerbread Victorians designed by Methodist settlers over a century ago, though the island has its share of redbrick colonials and vinyl-sided ranches. Like the houses, the population on the island is diverse, yet all share the experience of having burrowed in. Porch swings are plentiful, and at night yellow mosquito lights are left on above the kitchen door for latecomers and cats. Picket fences wind around the houses, drunkenly following the uneven terrain of the earth after years of rains and snows.

The lawns here are generally parched, bright green only after the rainy months of spring. The public golf course has stubborn dry patches on its green, and there are dandelions growing around the ninth hole. In September, autumn winds blow dry threads of black seaweed across the sandy beach. Whitecaps rush to shore in large, exciting waves. The water turns green and murky as the mud swells up from underneath. Not a single sun worshiper is left. All the children are gone, back to school, learning alphabets instead of playing in the sand. At night the skies are mysterious. But always the air is crisp. A person can think here. And plan her next move.

Warm weather brings visitors, energy, calm blue water and hot sun. The summer ferry brings weekenders from the mainland. Some come in cars, others ride bikes and carry backpacks. They are always hungry from the ride. On Saturday nights they go to dinner at the small hotel in town. Those who cannot get reservations go to Carol-Jean's Luncheonette. On the front lawn leading up to Carol-Jean's, two plastic pink flamingoes guard the front door where a line of waiting customers spills out, waiting for dinner. On Sunday morning, the brunch line is even longer. In the vestibule, a bulletin board announces church socials, lost dogs, and local property. Island groups are free to leave their literature on a small table: *Worried about Electromagnetic Radiation?*, *International Cesarean Awareness Network*, *Discovering Your Previous Lives.* There are local newspapers for sale, and Comfort Isle sweatshirts.

Inside, Carol-Jean's is all done up in red and white, like a bad valentine. The counter that runs the length of the place is bright red formica. The rest of the place is lined with clean white tiles, and there are white lace curtains on all the windows. Above the swinging doors leading to the kitchen, a sign says, *Welcome to Carol-Jean's.*

I've never bothered to change that sign, and now a lot of folks here call me Carol-Jean. I guess that's all right because it doesn't make anybody unhappy, and no matter what they call me they still come here for fried eggs and molasses biscuits in the morning, on their way to work or the beach. Besides, the backers own my name anyway.

My skills as a painter have finally come in handy. I advertise my specials on the wall above the counter with illustrations: Bulldozer Toast (a woman sitting on a yellow bulldozer eats a plate of french toast), Rancher's Delight Sandwich (the bread wears a ten-gallon hat), Caramel Dutch Apple Pie (the pie wears dancing clogs). We also serve a King Kong Tuna Melt, and the sign above the coffee pot reads, *We grind fresh each day.*

My friends know where I am. They visit or send letters or call. Frenchie still lives on Saint Marks Place, running Threads out of his own home. These days he dresses fewer drag queens, and he has expanded his work with singers. He still travels with The Babes. He sends postcards. There is never any message, just his signature, *your old friend, Frenchie.*

Rayburn Billy is building a solid practice in adolescent psychiatry in Brooklyn Heights. He visits on weekends every few months, though never in ballet season. He reads the Sunday paper and goes antiquing. Last time, he brought a young woman, and this time, a young man.

Ginger married her supervisor and they moved into his two-bedroom apartment. They hired a decorator, decided not to have children, and travel every chance they get. I speak to her once a week on the telephone.

As for debts paid and unpaid, Dolores married a sheep rancher in Argentina and sent me a Christmas card last winter: baby Jesus in the manger, lots of sparkling snow. My mother still hopes I'll come to my senses, though it was one of Lilly's old DuBuffets that bought me my luncheonette. Reluctant to part with it, but resigned, she helped me sell the painting to the highest bidder. "Come on, Lilly," I put on my best Gunnar imitation to convince her, "you know you want to," and I guess she did. My share of the quarterly profits from Kittridge's goes directly to Lilly, to pay off what I still owe her.

Fatima quadrupled her number of falafel carts and brought over her entire family from Egypt. Now they all sell falafels in Manhattan, Queens and Brooklyn. Since Fatima started buying out the rest of her uncle's business, Wally calls her the Triboro Threat. And, just recently, a small new gallery on the Lower East Side, housed in what was once a pirogi factory, took a few of Wally's pieces for a show this fall called "Portraits of Indescribable Things." It's nice to know that people, at least the ones I've known, manage to get what they want in life, or what they deserve.

Gunnar visits me whenever he can get away, reassured to find me in the same place. He visits for pleasure, not business. We talk about old times and what we might do if there are new times. He has his eye on the stately little Victorian next door. He is on very good terms with the old woman who lives there, and she has told him she will sell it to him next year when she moves in with her sister down the road. He is in no hurry, but he plans to turn the house into a bed and breakfast. Meanwhile, I make only small improvements: an awning and cafe tables so I can serve iced cappuccinos in the summer when people like to drink outdoors. Later, perhaps, I'll build a small addition with just enough shelving to sell pickles and relishes, locally made.

I spend my days flipping blueberry wheat cakes and turkey burgers on the grill. In the winter, I will close my shutters and go sailing around warmer islands, floating for a few months, no destination in mind. Gunnar joined me last year, perhaps he will again. Sometimes I think about starting up a little general store in a marina. The food isn't very good in the tropics, but who's hungry anymore?

My new life suits me. When the tourists begin to show up at Carol-Jean's at the beginning of each summer, they look like plucked chickens ready for a browning. When they sit down at my counter and order a slice of my fresh lemon meringue, they remind me of how it felt to be climbing hard and rising fast.

"Go ahead," I say, smiling. "Eat that pie and enjoy every bite of it. You deserve it." And if I'm not too busy, I like to stand still and watch them eat. It helps me to remember everything, the whole story, of how I landed here, and how I gave my heart to the restaurant business.

About the Author

Karen Hubert Allison is the former owner, with her husband Len Allison, of a three-star restaurant in New York City called Huberts. They and their children now live on Maui, where Karen is cooking up her next novel.